Dear Readers,

We've made a New Year's resolu— to bring
you the best in contemporary romance. Why not
make a resolution of your own and treat yourself
to a Bouquet today?

This month, Zebra, Bantam, and Love Spell
author Kate Holmes takes readers to a windswept
North Carolina beach, where a shy artist and a
world-weary photographer take the first steps toward love as they build **Sand Castles** . . . and a
beautiful future together. From veteran Zebra
author Clara Wimberly comes **Beneath A Texas
Moon,** a poignant story of one woman's second
chance at love with the man who taught her about
passion—a man who's about to learn he's the father of her child.

On the lighter side, **Dangerous Moves** is Mary
Morgan's look at how opposites attract, in which
a thrill-seeking cowboy decides to take his pretty
physical therapist for the ride of her life . . . for
good. Finally, beloved, prize-winning author Deb
Stover presents **A Matter of Trust,** the story of a
young doctor returning to her small hometown to
discover that the high school sweetheart who
broke her heart is still around—and eager to make
amends in the sweetest way.

So start your New Year off right . . . with four
breathtaking new love stories from Bouquet.

Kate Duffy
Editorial Director

FIRST LOVE RECAPTURED

He didn't have to think about his next move. It just seemed to happen. She felt so small in his arms, so delicate. So right. There was that familiar spark between them, one that tantalized with every touch, every look. Diego's body tightened. The old desire resurfaced, quick and urgent.

Jessica surprised even herself, snuggling against him with no hesitation, letting him soothe her and stroke her hair as if she were a child. He let his hands move down her back to the delicate curve of her spine. The remembrance of last night and the way she had kissed him, then retreated, came back in a rush. He didn't want to risk pushing her away again. . . .

BENEATH A TEXAS MOON

CLARA WIMBERLY

Zebra Books
Kensington Publishing Corp.
http://www.zebrabooks.com

ZEBRA BOOKS are published by

Kensington Publishing Corp.
850 Third Avenue
New York, NY 10022

Zebra and the Z logo Reg. U.S. Pat. & TM Off.

First Printing: January, 2000
10 9 8 7 6 5 4 3 2 1

Printed in the United States of America

ONE

The man pacing the marble floor outside an office in the state capitol complex could have posed for a Texas Ranger recruitment poster.

The well-known lone star badge gleamed against a sparkling white shirt. Neatly creased dark jeans encased the long, lean legs of the man pacing—three, four, five steps. He turned, repeated the sequence. Tan, obviously expensive boots, the same color as his shoulder holster, tapped out a restless rhythm and caused other visitors to glance nervously at the tall, dark Texan who slapped a white summer Stetson against his thigh as he paced.

"You may go in now, Ranger Serrat," the girl at the desk said.

The man stopped, raising his dark brows questioningly, as if he'd emerged from a daze. Beneath his scrutiny, the girl blushed and nodded to him.

"I said you can go in now," she repeated, and smiled.

"Thanks."

In the office, long windows threw light across the desk and over the shoulders of the man seated

behind it. The room reflected the West as it once
had been. An assortment of firearms, badges, and
sepia colored pictures of lean, tough-looking cow-
boys, all of them wearing variations of the Texas
Ranger badge, hung on the walls. The men pictured reflected a more old-fashioned version of the
Rangers, but all had the same cool, undaunted
look in their eyes—the same as the dark-eyed man
who'd just entered the office.

Faded letters on a tattered piece of material
spelled out an old Ranger motto: Ride like a Mexican, track like a Comanche, shoot like a Ken-
tuckian, and fight like the devil.

"Afternoon, Captain."

"Hey, Diego—good to see you." The man behind the desk stood up and extended his hand to
the younger man. "Have a seat. How's the shoulder?"

Diego's hand went automatically to his left shoulder as he rotated it forward.

"Passable," he said.

"A couple of inches further in the other direction and that bullet could have taken out one of
our best Rangers."

"Yeah. Well, it didn't. I'm still kickin'."

The captain frowned slightly, then picked up a
sheaf of papers and thumbed through them.

"You are aware that the doctor has released you
for limited duty only?"

Diego's lips moved impatiently as he leaned back
in the chair, stretched out his legs and crossed one

booted foot over the other. "I'd hoped you wouldn't hold me to that."

Captain Dave Byrd had hired Diego almost five years earlier. He was tough, but he also had a reputation for taking care of his men, even if he sometimes had to bend the rules a bit to do it.

"You're damned right I'm gonna hold you to it," the captain said. "Have to. The way things are now, hell, if I so much as sneeze, the press is here askin' me which cold medicine I'm taking. Just between you and me, I'm damned sick of it. Makes a man long for retirement."

Diego smiled, his straight white teeth flashing against the darkness of his skin.

"No disrespect intended, sir, but I find that hard to believe. You've been in this business too long. It gets to be a part of you."

"You're right about that. Been in it almost as long as you are old, I suspect." The captain grimaced wryly. He rubbed a hand through his thinning gray hair and inspected Diego with eyes grown weary over sixty-some-odd years of life.

"You know what they say," Diego drawled. "A Ranger can't quit, he just dies on his horse."

"Yeah, well, that was in the old days. Death in front of the computer would be more like it now." Byrd spoke with obvious disgust and flashed a look of disdain toward the keyboard and monitor on his desk.

The older man stood up and walked to the window. Diego sat silently, his earlier impatience controlled as he waited for the other man to speak.

"I know you're anxious to get back to work, and I have an assignment that could work for both of us. It ties in with a man we've been investigating. We finally have the chance to put him away for good."

"I'm listening," Diego said.

"Remember Lamar Colby?"

"Yeah, I remember him." Diego nodded. "Suspected of bringing drugs across the border and laundering money through legitimate businesses in different parts of Texas."

"For the past year or so, he's been operating out of El Paso. Got some shady friends over in Ciudad Juarez. We have a business associate out there, a big-time rancher, who wants to turn state's evidence against him."

Diego shrugged his shoulders and rubbed the back of his neck. A small tingle worked down his spine. He'd brought his mother here from El Paso. He hadn't been back since that summer when he'd said good-bye to Jessica.

But the words El Paso still evoked memories of his past and his struggle to make life better for himself and his family.

And then there was Jessica . . . always Jessica.

Shrugging away his uneasiness, he focused his attention on the captain.

"You think Colby might try and pay this man off?" Diego asked.

"Or kill him off."

Diego nodded. "Be kind of stupid, wouldn't it?"

"Colby's not stupid. But he is arrogant, and he

prides himself on his power. He's managed to elude the authorities for some time now. After we serve the warrant, just to make sure Mr. Colby doesn't pull anything funny, they've asked us to secure the witness's ranch, then stick around a while for guard duty. That's where you come in."

Diego shrugged his shoulders uncomfortably and nodded. His feelings of alarm grew stronger. Was it just the mention of El Paso? Or was it something more?

"The witness will pay for any security system we want installed and as many men as it takes to patrol. You'll be in charge of the operation, and you'll be staying at the hacienda, just in case anyone gets past the other stuff."

"All right."

"There's just one small hitch," Byrd said.

Diego turned the white Stetson around and around between his fingers.

"Yeah, I thought there might be." He took a deep breath, leaned back in the chair, and stretched his legs out in front of him.

"That's why you're such a good lawman, cowboy. Good instincts." Byrd's grin was more a grimace than a smile. Then his expression turned solemn. "You know the people you'll be protecting, Diego. It's Frank McLean and his daughter, Jessica."

Diego felt as if some giant vacuum had sucked every ounce of air out of his lungs.

Quickly he sat up and leaned forward in the chair, staring hard, his eyes glittering dangerously.

"Jessica? Old man McLean's involved her in this?"

Byrd raised his hand. "Look, I know you pretty well. You confided in me about your connection to the McLeans a long time ago. When this situation came up, I didn't want to throw you into it without knowing what was going on. If you'd rather I give the assignment to someone else, then—"

"No." Diego clenched his jaw. Damn Frank McLean. The man always had been a self-centered bastard, but to put his own daughter in jeopardy like this? "I'm not saying that. Is she all right?"

"From what I understand, she doesn't even know about it yet."

Diego closed his eyes and rubbed his forehead, where a dull ache had begun. "God."

"Seems McLean uncovered some questionable entries in some of Colby's paperwork about the same time they received notice that the attorney general's office would be conducting an audit of their business. McLean knows he could be implicated, and the only way out of possible prosecution is for him to testify against Colby. But before everything hits the fan, he's asked for protection for himself and his daughter."

Diego nodded. At least McLean had sense enough to do that.

"Matter of fact, he asked specifically for you."

Diego glanced up quickly, his eyes narrowing. "I wasn't exactly one of his favorite people."

"Well, it's true. Seems he's kept up with you

since you left. Here's the request with his signature. Read it for yourself."

Diego scanned the paper briefly and took a deep breath. Several reasons for refusing the assignment raced through his head, including the fact he'd be in the same house with Jessica for weeks. He didn't look forward to returning to a place where he'd always been looked down on as a half-breed and the son of a servant, a man unworthy of being in the company of the boss's daughter. And now McLean was asking for him?

"What are you thinking?"

"McLean's no fool. He's counting on my still having feelings for Jessica, perhaps even a certain loyalty to him, too. No other Ranger could bring that with him."

"And do you?" Byrd asked. "Still have feelings?"

"No." Diego moved his shoulders uncomfortably. "That was a long time ago."

The phone rang and Captain Byrd motioned Diego to stay.

"Yes?" Byrd said into the phone. "All right, I'll take the call."

While Byrd talked, Diego walked toward the window and looked down on the capitol grounds. From here he could see Coppini's statue of Terry's Rangers. He'd memorized the inscription years ago when he first came: "There is no danger of a surprise when the Rangers are between us and the enemy."

He'd made it his creed, and for the first time in his life he'd found his niche. The job had made him feel invincible and right about himself, something he needed to retain if he accepted this assignment.

Hell, who did he think he was fooling? Of course he would accept. There was no one he would trust with Jessica's safety except himself. He had loved her. He'd been her first love and she his. That summer he'd fooled himself into thinking it could last forever.

As he stood gazing down at the green trees that surrounded the capitol, Diego couldn't help remembering that time and place. He could see in his mind's eye those almond-shaped green eyes, rimmed by dark lashes, that hair tinted golden by the Texas sun—hair that smelled of sun and rain. He'd never known anyone like Jessica McLean, and he'd never completely forgotten her, no matter how hard he tried.

They'd made love for the first time beneath the cottonwood trees. Diego had been lost in those green eyes, so alive and warm, lost in the love and trust she gave to him so easily.

Her legs, strong and muscular from horseback riding—those long, beautiful legs had driven him crazy. In fact, everything about her had driven him crazy.

But it was more than that with Jessica. More than a body had attracted him to her. She had the heart and soul of an angel and a spirit as big as Texas. How many times in the past five years had he compared other women to her?

He had allowed himself to forget his mother was the McLeans' cook and his father a migrant farm worker who was often away. He even forgot that the girl who gave herself so readily and so completely was the daughter of one of West Texas's richest, most influential men. They'd been two young people in love, two people who couldn't seem to get enough of each other.

As a boy, sneered at by the world, Diego Serrat had learned to be cautious and to guard his feelings. With Jessica, he'd let his guard down. He'd allowed himself to be pulled into a dream that they were equals, just a boy and a girl who could overcome life's barriers and be together always.

Until the old man offered him money to leave and told him Jessica had admitted what a mistake she'd made.

"Fool," Diego muttered.

"Diego? Hey, cowboy."

Diego turned as Byrd's voice penetrated the fog that had wrapped around his mind.

"Thinking about the assignment?"

"Among other things." Diego raked his hand through his black hair.

"Well?"

"I want it."

"I thought you might." Byrd smiled wistfully. "You're a good man, Serrat. I hope I'm not getting you into something you'll regret."

"You're not, sir. I can handle it."

"I was hoping you'd say that."

TWO

Jessica felt as if she'd just fallen asleep when she heard a knock at her bedroom door. She groaned and rolled over, glancing at the clock beside the bed.

It was almost eight.

"Come in."

"Sorry to wake you, Miss Jessie." The dark-haired woman who stuck her head into the room was Rosie Blackwing, a Native American who had worked at the McLean ranch for years.

"It's all right, Rosie. I should have been up an hour ago."

"Your father asked me to take Tommy outside this morning. He wants you to meet him in the breakfast room as soon as possible."

Jessica frowned and kicked the sheets off her legs.

"Did he say what it's about?" Jessica and her father often had breakfast together, but Tommy was always included. Frank McLean adored his grandson and liked nothing better than spending time with him.

"No, he didn't." Rosie shrugged. "Sorry."

After Rosie left, Jessica pulled on a pair of gauzy moss green pants and a matching sleeveless shirt. She brushed her thick hair vigorously, the only way she could control it, then pulled it back, tying it with a green silk scarf.

When she came downstairs, her father was alone in the breakfast room. Long arched windows curved around one end of the room, affording a panoramic view of the Sierra Diablo Mountains to the southeast. This morning the mountains were purple against a clear blue summer sky. It was a sight Jessica never tired of seeing.

Frank McLean stood looking out the windows, his hands behind his back. He was tall and had always been a big man, but since his wife's death two years ago, he'd grown noticeably thinner. Until this moment, Jessica hadn't realized how thin and stooped he'd become.

She frowned and tried to shake off the odd feeling. Something was not right. There was an air of melancholy about him, almost defeat in the slump of his shoulders, as if he were very weary and troubled.

Was he sick? Was that what he wanted to talk to her about? Jessica's heart lurched at the thought of losing him so soon after her mother's death.

She'd seen this same discomfort in him last night when he mentioned problems with a business associate, but then he'd become hesitant and changed the subject.

"Dad, is something wrong?"

Frank McLean turned and smiled. Jessica couldn't remember seeing him smile much when she was young. He had been driven by ambition, often too busy for what he considered the trivialities of a wife and young daughter. Secretly Jessica had always suspected he would have preferred a son instead of a daughter. Maybe that was why he was so crazy about Tommy. Her mother had said the boy's birth had mellowed Frank McLean and made him realize there was more to life than accumulating wealth and power.

Perhaps that should have made Jessica resentful. After all, that mellowing was something neither she nor her mother could accomplish. But she was pleased he cared so much for his grandson. Tommy needed a father figure in his life, and that was the main reason she had remained here at the ranch—for her son.

"Come in, sweetheart," her father said. "We have fresh strawberries this morning, your favorite." He motioned toward the small table, beautifully set with cream-colored linen and colorful southwestern earthenware dishes.

Jessica had to make herself sit quietly and eat, knowing it wouldn't do to rush her father into whatever he wanted to tell her. He barely touched his food, but still she waited.

"Honey," he said, finally putting down his fork. He was frowning and couldn't seem to meet her questioning gaze. "I mentioned last night I have a problem with one of the warehouse businesses in El Paso."

"Yes."

"One of our bookkeepers found some puzzling entries in one of our ledgers just before the state came and conducted an audit. It might not have been noticed if we hadn't been preparing for that. Did I tell you this?"

Jessica frowned. It wasn't like him to be forgetful. He seemed so old this morning—feeble, even.

"No, I don't think you did."

"Yes, well . . . it was a few weeks ago."

"What kind of puzzling entries?"

He sighed and rose to walk to the windows.

"Rather substantial amounts of money were coming in without explanation or backup documentation, and none of it was anything I was familiar with."

"Where was the money coming from?"

"Supposedly Colby's business at the granary. But it was too much money to make any sense. Way too much."

Jessica took a deep breath. She'd had a feeling the problem was Colby all along. "Did you ask him about it?"

"Yeah." Frank McLean rubbed his chin as he turned to face his daughter. "And I told him we were about to be audited."

"What did he say?"

"Something along the lines of 'just keep your mouth shut and let me take care of it.' "

"Oh, Daddy," she whispered. She could see her father's apprehension, and she couldn't stop the terror that raced through her.

"It's all right, though, baby." He sat at the table and took her hand. "I've thought about it long and hard. You know I've done a few things in my life I'm not proud of. But this was something I couldn't let go on, not right under my nose in a business I'd built from top to bottom. If I let Colby take care of it, I'd be no better than he is."

"I never liked him. Mother didn't like him, either."

"I know. I know." He sighed and shook his head. "But your mother was ill and I couldn't think straight. I never gave her the time she wanted when she was healthy. With her dying—I'd be damned if I was going to abandon her then. I needed a partner who could take the ball and run with it, someone who could help me diversify. I should have checked him out more thoroughly, but I didn't." He shrugged his shoulders and his eyes glittered oddly.

"It's all right, Dad. Everything will work out, especially if you do the right thing. What can I do to help?"

"Honey, I'm grateful, but it's gone way beyond something you can help me with." He looked straight into her eyes, his gaze pleading for her understanding. "That's what I wanted to talk to you about this morning. It's gone way beyond my control."

"What? Please, just tell me, Dad."

"The state found the discrepancies before I could do anything, and they didn't believe I was an innocent bystander. Not that I wouldn't have done the right thing anyway, but in order to avoid prosecution myself, I have no choice. I can't keep quiet about what I know."

"They want you to testify against Colby?" Jessica's eyes widened in alarm. "But, Dad, you know his reputation. He's ruthless. There's probably nothing he wouldn't do to protect himself."

"It's all right. We'll beef up our security system here, hire some men to patrol the fences, put in cameras. And I've asked for protection, someone to be with you and Tommy at all times."

"You've hired a bodyguard? Who?"

"Well now, honey, that's the real reason I had to talk to you first thing this morning. You see, the man assigned to the case is already here."

He walked to the door, and Jessica stood up, staring at him as she tried to understand why he was being so mysterious.

"You can come in now," she heard him say.

The man who stepped through the door was an awesome sight. He was tall and lanky in well-fitting jeans. A silver badge gleamed against his sparkling white dress shirt. Jessica's gaze moved from the weapon he wore in a shoulder holster up to his face.

Then she looked into his eyes . . . beautiful, familiar eyes, as black as the darkest Texas night. Eyes she once knew so well.

Jessica thought her heart might stop beating. She gasped and reached backward for her chair.

Diego's eyes, dark and impenetrable, bore into

hers, and his familiar gaze made Jessica tremble from head to toe.

"What are you doing here?" Jessica turned toward her father, seeking an explanation. All she got was his rather sheepish expression. "What have you done?" she asked.

How could he put her in this position, spring this on her unannounced? Did he intend letting Diego learn about Tommy this way—learn he had a son she'd kept from him all this time—without giving her a chance to explain first?

She swallowed hard and took a deep breath, then turned to stare at Diego again.

He'd changed. His hair was shorter, sexier, and the clothes he wore were obviously more expensive than her Diego could have afforded. But his eyes were as deep and dark, as beautiful and mysterious as ever. He was taller, broader through the chest and shoulders, and there was a coolness in him she didn't remember. There was no smile, no welcome in his look or in his voice. She couldn't see the slightest hint of the young man she'd known so long ago.

She felt trapped in the moment, wanting it to go on forever, and yet wanting to escape it, too.

"Well," Diego said, his voice deep and steady. "I take it your father didn't tell you I was coming." He glanced quickly and rather disdainfully toward her father.

"No."

"I'm sorry, honey. I asked for Diego specifically. I knew I could trust him." Her father's gaze was

pleading, saying what he couldn't say out loud—
that he knew Diego would have more reason to
want to protect them once he learned it involved
the life of his own son.

"And from the look on your face, I suspect he
didn't tell you because he knew you'd say no,"
Diego said in a cool drawl.

For a moment she wanted to cry at the awkwardness and this new coolness between them. Once
she had felt so close to him, and there was a time
when he would not have held anything back. Despite his distrust of most people, when it came to
Jessica, they had loved and laughed with the sweet
abandon of youth.

Jessica shook her head, staring at her father.
How could he do this to her? But it was typical
of what Frank McLean had always done. He
thought it was his God-given right to have things
his way or to manipulate a situation for his own
benefit. He'd made this decision on his own from
the very beginning, from being a witness against
Colby to calling in the Rangers to protect his
ranch and his family, but Jessica never dreamed
he would use her son in the process.

At least he had the decency to look away from
her in shame.

"Mr. McLean," Diego said, "could you give us
a few minutes alone?"

Frank McLean looked at Jessica and she nodded.
Without a word, he turned and left the room.

Diego watched McLean go, then turned his cool,
appraising gaze on Jessica.

She'd changed. When he'd first met Jessica, she was an awkward, trusting kid who followed him around, watching him with adoring amber-flecked eyes. When he returned from college, he'd found a beautiful young woman who had declared she would never love anyone else, and he had fallen in love, as well.

But that was all changed now.

It was obvious she wasn't pleased to see him.

Yet he found her more beautiful than ever. Her beauty was more sedate, but with an underlying sensuality that made him want to loosen the scarf from her shining hair and pull her into his arms. Even now, after preparing himself for this moment, his first instinct was to touch her, to just once let his fingers caress her soft skin.

Diego frowned and shook his head, trying to free himself of those unwanted thoughts. That wasn't why he was here, and thinking that way wouldn't help Jessica or himself.

"I don't want you here." She'd been watching him, wondering at the thoughts behind those appraising black eyes, and trying not to let him see just how disconcerted she was by his presence or his looks.

"That's obvious," he drawled. "The question is why. It's been a long time. Surely whatever happened between us is forgotten. After all, we were just kids."

"Why?" She found she couldn't quite meet his gaze. She turned away from him, crossing her

arms over her breasts and walking to the windows.
"Why?"

God, what could she say? How was she going to
handle this? Possibilities raced through her head.
Perhaps she could send Tommy away until this was
over. Or should she just blurt out everything to
Diego now and let the chips fall where they would?

She shook her head. She couldn't decide right
now how she would tell him he was a father or
how she would explain why she'd kept his son
from him. She needed some time alone to think
and to decide what was best for Tommy . . . and
for her.

It angered her that her father had done this
purposely so she would be forced to tell Diego
about his son. She suspected it was what he had
wanted all along. Even though he'd never ap-
proved of Diego, he'd often said a man should
know about his own son.

And Frank McLean always got his way.

Suddenly Jessica felt the rage that often sim-
mered within her—rage because of the way her
life had turned out, rage that no one ever seemed
to consider her or what she wanted.

"Look at me, Jess." Diego's voice was deceptively
soft. "Why can't you just look at me? I understand
this is awkward for you. It isn't easy for me, either,
coming back here to this house."

Jessica turned and looked at him then, into his
eyes. She was surprised at how easily he expressed
himself. That hadn't always been so. Back then he
would withdraw inside himself when he was con-

fronted with emotional issues. He couldn't seem
to help running away, just as he'd run away from
her and the love she offered that summer so long
ago.

But there was no way he could have known he
was also running out on his own child. She'd
made certain of that. So why should she resent
him for something he couldn't have known? She
knew her thoughts were unreasonable and confus-
ing, but she couldn't seem to help it.

He might have hated emotional issues, but he'd
been supremely confident about his masculinity
and his sexuality. He'd been proud of his Indian
and Hispanic ancestry, even arrogant about it at
times. But perhaps she was one of the few people
who knew just how little confidence he'd had in
his ability and his future.

Obviously, his success had given him that confidence. He seemed harder, his pride even fiercer
than before.

"Since you find it so uncomfortable being here,
I'm surprised you came. Why didn't you just tell
them to send someone else?"

Diego grunted and shook his head. *Who else
could protect you the way I can?* he wanted to ask.

But he didn't. Instead he smiled slowly, the smile
not quite reaching his eyes.

"I'm staying, Jess, so get used to it. I'll try to
stay out of your way, make this as painless as possible for both of us. If it will make you more comfortable, I can stay in the background, like a
servant. I know how it's done, after all. Everything

will be just as before . . . except for one obvious difference, of course."

Her face burned as he reminded her of their passion and the fact that they hadn't been able to get enough of one another.

"Now, if you'll excuse me, I believe someone is waiting to show me to my room. Seems I'll be staying in *el patron's* house this time instead of in my old room behind the barn—more convenient, in case the princess needs me for anything." His voice dripped with sarcasm.

She found herself wanting to rage at him, wanting the battle to continue instead of having him walk away from her with such arrogant coolness.

"You're still as damned sarcastic and bitter as ever, I see."

His eyes narrowed and the smile left his face. "Baby," he said quietly, "you don't know the half of it."

She gritted her teeth and counted to ten. "Shall I make arrangements for you to have your meals in your room?"

He raised his brows and his dark eyes sparkled. "Oh, no. I'm looking forward to having dinner with Boss McLean and his princess—finally."

"Give that old dog a rest, Diego." She forced a short laugh. "It doesn't make me feel guilty anymore, and your presence hardly shakes me the way it used to, either."

If he only knew what a lie *that* was. "I'm a grown woman used to being on my own, not that silly little girl with stars in her eyes who followed you around just waiting to be tossed a crumb, so don't think I'm going to scurry out of your way every time you come near."

His black, mysterious gaze met her sparkling green one. For a moment they challenged one another, the tension in the air between them almost alive.

But despite her bravado, Jessica's heart drummed in her chest and an unexplained shiver raced down her back.

"I don't need anyone to decide what's best for me anymore. In fact, I've taken over all the duties my mother once had. I make decisions about crops, livestock, and investments." She didn't really know why she was telling him this. He could probably care less.

"Is that a fact?" He smiled. "Well, I'm certainly impressed," he added wryly.

She shook her head. This sparring was making her nervous and anxious and getting her nowhere. What she really needed was to get away from him and decide what to do about Tommy.

Just then the door to the dining room burst open and the decision was made for her.

Tommy barreled into the room in his usual exuberant way. As if in a slow-moving dream, she saw Diego turn, saw him watch the young boy race past and throw his arms around her legs.

"Mom, guess what? There's a new colt just borned. Want to come see it?" He grasped her hand and looked up at her, following her gaze. Only then did he realize someone else was in the room.

He stared up at Diego curiously, and his small arms tightened around Jessica's legs.

She put her arm around Tommy's shoulder, pulling him closer against her, as if she could protect him from what was to come.

She looked at Diego and swallowed hard. Her legs were trembling so badly she thought they might not hold her.

He was looking at her with stormy, questioning eyes, a look that turned her insides to jelly. His head was cocked curiously to one side and there was a small frown line at the bridge of his nose as he stared first at her, then down into Tommy's eyes. His gaze flickered oddly, and he seemed troubled and eerily still as he stared at the boy whose eyes were so black and curious . . . and so very much like his own.

THREE

Tommy's eyes were bright with curiosity as he looked up at the tall man with the shiny badge.

Diego stooped down, his hips resting against his heels as he put himself at eye level with the boy.

"Hey," he said softly.

Guilelessly, Tommy moved forward, resting his small body against Diego's knees. His chubby hand moved forward, almost touching the silver badge, then stopping as he glanced around to his mother, then back at Diego.

Seeing Diego and Tommy together sent a fierce, bittersweet pain ripping through Jessica's heart. She bit her lips to quell the sob that rose unbidden in her throat.

"It's OK. You like the badge? Most kids do. You can touch it if you like." Diego leaned closer to Tommy and let him reach out and touch the gleaming star.

Jessica found it hard to believe this was the same man who had chilled her with his cool indifference. The gruffness in his voice was gone, replaced by a tenderness and gentleness she remembered all too well.

With every sense she possessed, she remembered. It began with an ache that started in her chest and spread like quicksilver through her entire body.

"What's your name, son?"

Tommy settled himself against Diego's thigh and his arm rested naturally on Diego's arm. Her son had always been outgoing and friendly, but this was different. It was as if he'd known Diego all his life.

How many times had she wondered—daydreamed, really—about the possibility of this moment, about what would happen if Diego one day walked through the door? She'd wondered if he would know instinctively, like a lion knows his cub, that Tommy belonged to him.

Her heart pounded as she waited for the answer to those questions.

"My name's Tommy."

"Well, hey, Tommy. My name is Diego." He reached out for Tommy's hand.

Without hesitation Tommy placed his small hand in Diego's.

"De-eggo?" He gave a high-pitched giggle.

Diego laughed, too, his white teeth flashing, his eyes glittering with genuine delight. The sound of their laughter together made Jessica's knees go weak, and she sank onto a nearby chair.

She knew exactly where this was heading. It was inevitable. There could be no turning back now.

The decision of how to tell Diego about his son was being taken away from her, and there was not a thing she could do about it.

The man she had once loved was no fool. He would know instinctively that Tommy was his son. He probably already did.

"How old are you, Tommy?"

Jessica held her breath, waiting.

"Four." Tommy held up his hand, spreading his fingers proudly to show Diego his age.

The laughter in Diego's eyes quickly disappeared and his gaze flickered toward Jessica. The muscles in his jaw worked as he clenched and unclenched his teeth. For a long moment he stared hard into her eyes, his look puzzled and accusing.

Jessica bit her lower lip to stop its trembling. Then she stood up and moved away from him . . . away from those incredible eyes that seemed to see into her very soul. She went to the windows that faced the Sierra Diablo Mountains, clutching her arms across her breasts as if she might anchor herself against a quick-moving storm.

He knew. He was too astute, too instinctual not to have known the moment he saw Tommy. They were so much alike.

But it had happened so suddenly that Jessica could hardly grasp what it meant for all of them.

She'd thought about this moment a million times, wanting to tell him and yet unable to. She'd never known how to tell him, and she'd begun to hope she'd never have to.

She continued to stand at the window, listening

to the conversation between Diego and Tommy. She smiled wistfully at some of Tommy's questions, her lips trembling at the thoughtful responses Diego gave. Her eyes filled with tears against her will. Angrily, she blinked them away.

Why should I feel guilty? she wanted to shout. He hadn't wanted her. Diego had left so easily, as if that life-changing summer meant nothing to him, as if he didn't know he'd been her whole life, or that in him she'd found everything she'd ever wanted.

She had no reason to think he would feel differently about her child.

"Mommy?"

She turned to Tommy, not letting her eyes meet Diego's.

"Can we take him to see the new colt?"

Before she could answer, Diego spoke.

"Tell you what, sport. I need to talk to your mom for just a minute. Why don't you and your grandpa go on out to the barn? I'll bet the colt is anxious to see you."

When Tommy frowned, Diego laughed and reached out to push a strand of dark hair out of his son's eyes. "I'll be along soon."

"You won't forget, will you?"

"I won't forget." Diego's quiet laugh was spontaneous and joyous.

Tommy's face brightened, and when he turned to look at Jessica, she thought her heart might actually explode with the love she felt for him.

"Will you come, too, Mom?"

"You bet I will, sweetheart." She forced herself to smile at him and Diego. The last thing she wanted was for her little boy to pick up on the tension that sparked between her and Diego, if he hadn't already.

Diego watched silently as Tommy left the room, his dark eyes filled with an odd, hungry longing. When the door closed, everything changed. The air seemed charged with electricity. Jessica took a deep breath and faced him.

"You want to tell me what I'm thinking isn't true?" he asked, his voice as cold as his eyes.

"How can I know what you're thinking? I never could manage that." She didn't know why she gave such a flip answer, except that she wasn't ready to face his accusations.

In two quick steps he was in front of her, towering over her. His hands grasped her arms and he shook her once, his teeth gritted in fury, his eyes glittering dangerously.

"No more games, Jessica," he growled. "No more!"

Her hands were against his shirt, and for a moment all she could do was stare at them. They seemed oddly delicate against his broad chest. It seemed strange to stand so close to him, to feel the strength and warmth of his body, smell the heady scent of his aftershave. For a moment she stood stunned and speechless.

Her gaze slid from her hands to his face, which was dark with anger.

"Damn you," he whispered, his voice hoarse

with emotion. "Damn you for keeping my son from me all these years. My God, how could you do it? Did you hate me so much?"

Jessica reached up to push him away, but instead she clung to his shirt, thinking oddly that she was wrinkling the neatly starched material. Her face contorted and she closed her eyes, shaking her head in mute sorrow at the pain in his voice.

"He is mine, isn't he?" he demanded, shaking her again. "Tell me, Jessica, or I swear—"

"Yes," she whispered. "Yes, Tommy is your son. Of course he is. How could he belong to anyone else?" She heard her words, and yet they seemed to come from someone else.

She pulled away from him and walked to the breakfast table, her hands trembling so badly she could barely manage to pour the juice from its earthenware carafe. She could still feel the imprint of his hands on her arms.

"In God's name, why have you done this? Why didn't you tell me? And why would you deny your son a father?"

"I'm . . . I'm sure there was a time when I could have given you several answers to that question." Tears swam in her eyes. "But now, seeing you face-to-face, I swear I can't think of a single one."

Diego made a sound of distrust deep in his throat.

"Well, you'd damned well better think of one. I'm not leaving until you explain this to me. Right now."

"I . . . I don't know what to say."

"Try a little honesty this time. You knew then and you know now." Anger seethed in his words. "It's still the same reason, isn't it, Jess? It's the name Serrat—the name of a half-breed, a nothing in the eyes of a high and mighty McLean."

"No." Jessica gasped at the pain and anger directed toward her.

"Don't deny it. My grandparents' Irish, Indian, and Hispanic blood isn't acceptable to you and your father. It wouldn't do for Tommy to be a mixed breed like his dad, would it? I was no more to your father than a mongrel pup that wandered onto his property, and just about as damned welcome. He couldn't let everyone in El Paso learn someone like that was actually Tommy's father."

Jessica shook her head, her eyes filled with pain as she tried to deny his words.

"So what *did* you tell the country club set, Jess? What lie did you and Frank McLean spin to explain away that little boy's parentage?"

"How can you accuse me of that?" she cried. "It isn't true. None of it. I never felt that way about you, Diego. Deep down inside you know that. It's what you always wanted to believe, and you wore it like a shield, but it's never been true."

Jessica shook her head, closing her eyes and wishing she could shut out the pain deep in his beautiful eyes.

"I never *wanted* to believe it. It was just there—a fact of life."

"You're wrong," she whispered.

"Then what other reason can you give me?"

Jessica said nothing and Diego made a quiet noise of disgust.

"My father died two years ago, Jessica." His voice broke in a raspy whisper.

"I . . . I'm sorry. I . . . I didn't know."

He didn't acknowledge her words.

"Do you know what he would have given for a chance to see this little boy, his only grandson? Do you?" He took a menacing step toward her.

But Jessica stood her ground, although every instinct within her warned her to run. Her head came up and she stared, her eyes glittering into his.

"I *am* sorry," she whispered, "whether you want to believe it or not."

"Sorry?" he asked, his voice incredulous. "You stole four years of life from me and my son, and all you can say is you're sorry? God, I'm looking at you, Jess, and I see the same bright eyes, the same beautiful face as the girl I used to know, but I swear I don't know you. I don't know you at all."

"What else can I do? I was wrong, but I can't bring back those years for you, Diego. I can't change anything that happened. All I can do is say I'm profoundly sorry and ask you to forgive me."

"Forgive you?" His hands went to his hips and he frowned, shaking his head and staring at her as if she were insane. "Are you serious?"

"I know it's a lot to expect—" She stopped, her voice cracking.

"You're damned right it's a lot to expect."

He stared at her for a long moment, his dark eyes narrowed, his teeth clenched tightly. His entire body was tense, his fists stiff by his side. Then slowly, imperceptibly, his expression changed, becoming cold and unyielding.

"Everything's always been so easy for you, hasn't it, Jess? Whatever you wanted, whatever you needed, all you had to do was snap your fingers." He shook his head. "You know, I always wondered how that would feel—having everyone's unqualified acceptance, knowing all I had to do was—"

"Please, Diego, don't."

"Oh, no, it's not going to be as easy as that, Jess. Your pleas and your tears might have moved me once, but not this time, baby. Not by a damned long sight."

FOUR

When the door opened and Rosie Blackwing stepped inside, Jessica's sigh of relief was almost audible.

"Mr. Serrat's room is ready now." Rosie turned slightly toward Diego, unable to contain a grin of delight. "Welcome back, Mr. Serrat," she said, her nod shy.

"Mr. Serrat, nothing." Diego took two long strides to where Rosie stood, then stooped and wrapped the slender woman in his arms, swinging her around until her feet flew off the floor. "You can hardly call a man mister once you've swatted him across the backside with a broom." He laughed.

Jessica blinked as she watched the scene before her. She could hardly believe how quickly he could change. One moment he was so angry at her she thought he might like to strangle her; the next he was completely disarming Rosie with his quick grin and impetuous charm.

Rosie giggled with delight. When Diego put her

down, she patted his shoulder as if he were still a
little boy.

"I never swatted you very hard." She wagged a
finger at him. "But you were always pilfering food
from the kitchen."

"I was a growing boy." Diego gave an exagger-
ated shrug of his broad shoulders.

Rosie nodded, her dark eyes moving over him
appreciatively.

"Well, I'm mighty happy to see how that hungry
boy grew into a very handsome man. You look
wonderful, Diego." Once again, she ducked her
head shyly.

"Why, thank you, Rosie." Diego was smiling, but
as soon as he glanced toward Jessica, his eyes grew
cool again.

"Rosie, why don't you go ahead and show Diego
to his room? I'll be in the barn with Tommy."
Jessica barely let her eyes meet Diego's.

"I'll join you in just a few minutes." His look
told her she wasn't going to get away from him
as easily as that.

She hurried from the room, conscious of his
dark gaze upon her, even more conscious of his
seething anger.

What was she going to say to him? She'd loved
him more than life itself, and his rejection had
devastated her. But she was hardly prepared or in-
clined to make that admission. Nor could she admit that, yes, part of the reason she'd kept Tommy
from him was to punish him for the hurt he'd
caused.

Today, facing the issue, it sounded so immature, so small-minded and ugly. Somehow over the years she'd justified her actions. But now, seeing the anger and pain in Diego's eyes, she couldn't believe she'd done it, or that five years had passed with this terrible secret in her heart and on her conscience.

She shook away her thoughts and hurried outside. As she walked, her trembling legs grew steadier. She needed to feel the warm Texas wind on her face and smell the clean scent of the desert air, get her thoughts together.

It was a beautiful morning—the sky clear and blue, a hint of a breeze barely stirring the leaves of the rosebushes near the house. The wind released the scent of roses into the air. For a moment, Jessica felt an ache in her heart for all she had lost.

The smell was sweet and poignant, and when she wasn't on guard, it reminded her so much of Diego and their exciting, forbidden nights together that it brought an ache to her chest.

She groaned softly and hurried toward the barn. Was there nowhere she could go to escape the look of betrayal she'd seen in his eyes? Now that he was here, would even the beautiful surroundings fail to soothe and comfort her?

As she walked into the barn, she heard Tommy's voice, soft, but filled with excitement.

She smiled as she approached him and her father.

"Mom, Mom," Tommy said. "Look at him. He's

up! He's walking!" Tommy laughed aloud as the colt floundered and toppled over into the straw-covered stall, then pushed himself up on his knees to try again.

"So I see."

Tommy glanced around, then frowned.

"Where is he? That man who came?"

"Rosie is showing Diego to his room. He should be here any moment now. Don't worry," she added. "He hasn't forgotten his promise."

Jessica glanced uneasily into her father's eyes. She was still angry with him, but his look of chagrin made her feel as if she should be apologizing to him.

"I'm sorry, sweetheart. I know how angry you must be with me," he said. "But I knew if I told you, you never would have allowed it. And I think you know, whether you're willing to admit it or not, that he's the best one to protect you and Tommy."

Jessica sighed and pushed her hair back from her face.

"My head knows you're right." She touched her hand briefly, softly to her heart, shaking her head mutely. "I also know it's past time for both of them to know the truth." She kept her voice low, watching Tommy to make sure he didn't catch on to the topic of their conversation.

"I didn't intend for it to go on this long, but . . ." She reached out and touched her son's dark hair and her eyes glittered with tears. "When they met, seeing the look on his face"—she nodded toward Tommy—"Dad, his excitement was a shock to me. I guess I hadn't realized how much he misses having a . . . you know . . ."

"Having a what?" Tommy asked, looking up at Jessica. There was a slight frown between his brows.

Someone entered the barn and Jessica turned around to see Diego walking slowly toward them. She wondered how long he'd been there . . . how much he'd heard.

"Diego!" Tommy shouted. Impulsively, he ran to the tall man and caught his hand, pulling him forward. "You came."

"Well sure I did, sport. I said I would. When a Ranger gives his word, it's as good as done."

Tommy's eyes grew large and he glanced up at his mother as if Diego's words had impressed him.

"That's right." She forced herself to smile, but she couldn't meet Diego's steely gaze.

Tommy laughed and began chattering about the colt.

"I have some papers to attend to," Frank McLean said. "When you're done here, come to my office, both of you, and we'll go over the security arrangements. Take your time."

After her father left, Jessica stepped back into the shadows, leaning against a post. For long moments she watched Tommy and Diego, letting herself be completely ignored. But for once, that feeling was not unwelcome.

She didn't want to talk to Diego just now, didn't

want to be the object of his penetrating look. She
certainly didn't want his wrath focused on her.

She needed time to adjust not only to the fact
that he knew Tommy was his son, but to his being
here. Despite what she'd told her father about it
being time to expose her secret, she wasn't prepared. In one quick, heart-stopping moment, Diego had stepped into their world. The moment
she saw him, she knew her life would be changed
forever.

She found it amazing how quickly Tommy and
Diego seemed to bond. Under other circumstances, Jessica would have found that the most
wonderful thing in the world. But now, knowing
Diego's anger with her, it made her anxious and
afraid.

What if he tried to take Tommy away from her,
to punish her for what she'd done? At the very
least, he could try to turn Tommy against her.

"I think we should go speak with your father."

For a moment, Jessica didn't hear Diego. When
the words finally penetrated her troubled mind,
she found him watching her. He was close, too
close, leaning against the stall beside her.

She could feel the warmth of his body, smell the
sexy scent of his aftershave.

She stepped away as if she'd gotten too close to
a hot flame.

Amusement played across his handsome features
as he studied her, his look knowing and alert.

"We have a lot of work to do. The sooner we

have the security system in place, the sooner the warrant can be issued for Colby's arrest," he said.

"Yes, yes, of course. I was lost in thought, I guess . . . just thinking about—"

His lips twisted sarcastically. "You have a lot to think about, don't you? But don't worry. I won't demand answers right now. Certainly not in our present company." He nodded toward Tommy, who was still lost in his admiration of the new colt.

"I suppose I should be grateful for small favors," she snapped.

"Yeah." His eyes turned stormy. "You should be. I could make this much worse for you, if I wanted to." His voice was soft . . . warning.

Jessica clamped her teeth together, staring into his eyes before whirling away from him and moving toward the entrance.

"Tommy," she said, glancing over her shoulder, "it's time to go, sweetie. I'm sure Rosie has your lunch ready."

"Oh, Mom." His body sagged exaggeratedly. "Do we have to? Can't I stay if Diego stays with me?"

"Mind your mom." Diego reached out and touched Tommy's shoulders. Immediately the boy responded, falling into step beside Diego. "We'll have plenty of time to watch the colt later. Besides, the poor little guy probably needs some lunch and a rest, too, just like you."

"After lunch, can we come back?" Tommy asked.

Diego glanced at Jessica.

"We'll talk about it," Jessica said. She waited at the door for Tommy, ignoring Diego as best she could.

But she was finding that more and more difficult to do with each passing moment.

He still affected her, damn him.

And as much as she hated herself for it, she couldn't seem to stop her eyes from looking into his, couldn't make herself ignore the way his lean hips and thighs looked in those jeans or the way his shirt stretched across his muscular shoulders and chest.

She closed her eyes and tried to shake away such unwanted thoughts. Taking Tommy by the hand, she pulled him with her toward the house.

When they met later in her father's study, Jessica positioned herself in a chair to the side and slightly away from Diego. As he and her father talked, she watched him, noting the easy way he discussed such things as motion sensors, video cameras, and high-tech security measures she'd never heard of.

He was confident without being cocky. For a moment, she felt proud. He had come so far, had turned himself into this self-assured, dauntless man who seemed to fear nothing. He certainly was not intimidated by Frank McLean.

The days of being a servant's son were far behind him. He spoke to his former employer now as an equal, and yet there seemed to be no consciousness of it on his part.

She found herself wondering about his life. What he had done these past five years? Had he married? Come close, even? Did he have other children?

That thought made Jessica sit up straighter in the chair. Her eyes opened wide as she glanced at his hands. She'd already noticed earlier that he wore no wedding ring. But had he ever?

"Jessica?" Her father laughed. When she glanced up, he and Diego were watching her.

"Yes?" she answered, red faced and flustered.

"Is that all right with you?"

She swallowed hard and shrugged her shoulders. "Is what all right?"

"I'll be moving into Tommy's room," Diego answered. "We can convert the playroom into his bedroom. That way the only entry to his room will be through mine. I'll be between your room and his, with adjoining doors between all three rooms."

Jessica bit her lower lip and frowned. Diego hadn't asked if it would be all right. In his supremely confident way, he had just said he was going to do it.

That didn't trouble her nearly as much as the fact he would be so close, with only a door separating them.

"I don't know if I like the idea of Tommy's being that far away from me," she said. "Is this really necessary?"

"Yes, it is." Diego's expression was serious. "Lamar Colby is a dangerous man, Jess, with power and money to burn. There's nothing he wouldn't do to keep from going to jail, including threatening Tommy."

"If he's that dangerous, won't we need more than one man to protect us, even if that man is one of the famous Texas Rangers?" She didn't know why she added that last sarcastic bit. It wasn't necessary.

But Diego only smiled. "They're already in place. Not even your regular hands know which of the new hires are Rangers."

"Sounds as if you have everything covered." Frank McLean rose from behind his desk.

When Diego stood, Frank reached out his hand.

"Thank you, Diego. Your coming here means more to me than you'll ever know. If it isn't against some kind of law, I'd like to compensate you for your—"

"Keep your money, McLean." Diego's face was hard, his eyes cold. "I don't want it or need it." He ignored Frank's hand and turned to retrieve his hat before walking out the door.

Jessica looked into her father's eyes. He shrugged his shoulders as if Diego's rejection hadn't bothered him, but she knew it had. For some reason, he wanted Diego to like him now. Jessica found his lack of perception sad.

She didn't know if her father had seen it or not, but she certainly had. That old resentment, that old bitterness was still alive in Diego. Beneath his confident surface, this handsome man still seethed with resentment.

She might not understand all his reasons, but she didn't much blame him.

Oddly enough, that hint of vulnerability made her want to reach out to him, made her long to hold him and comfort him and tell him he was worth more than any man she'd ever known.

But how could she expect him to believe that after what she'd done?

FIVE

Diego didn't return for lunch. Although Jessica's first reaction was one of relief, she felt a certain disappointment, as well—not that she was looking forward to the inevitable confrontation between them.

But despite everything, the truth was she couldn't keep herself from wanting to see him.

"Well, where did he go?" Frank McLean asked when Rosie informed them of Diego's absence.

"All he said was he was going for a walk," Rosie said as she served the soup. "Cook packed a lunch for him and he took off, just like when he was a boy."

"Does he plan on being here for dinner?" Jessica asked.

Rosie shrugged. Jessica told herself at least she'd have the afternoon to think of what to say to him. But when he didn't return for dinner, either, she was surprised.

That night, it was past midnight when she pushed the sheets off her legs and got out of bed. She'd tried everything to help herself fall asleep, from filling her room with flickering candles to taking a long, warm bath. Nothing worked.

She'd lain in bed for what seemed like hours, listening for sounds from the next room. She'd even imagined the door bursting open and Diego standing there with a murderous look on his face, demanding his explanation.

Hurriedly, Jessica threw off her nightgown and crossed the dark room. She pulled on soft faded jeans and a cotton sweater and slid her feet into well-worn sandals.

Here on the second floor, each room had French doors which led onto a balcony. The balcony overlooked an enclosed courtyard surrounded on all four sides by the sprawling Spanish-style house.

Jessica opened the doors quietly and let herself out, lifting her face to the pale moonlight and breathing in the scent of jasmine and roses that hung from the balcony trellis.

There were no lights in the room next door, and she wondered again where Diego could be. Was this some kind of game he was playing? Something to make her suffer? Or was it something else, something more serious?

The thought that Diego could be hurt or lost in the desert sent a shudder coursing raggedly through her body.

"You shouldn't be out here alone."

"Oh!" She turned toward the other balcony. Diego pushed himself away from the wall and out of the shadows of the house, where he'd obviously been watching her all along.

"Good heavens, you almost frightened me out of my mind. What are you doing out here? Spying on me?"

"Hardly," he drawled. "Couldn't sleep. How about you?"

"No, I . . . I had been asleep, but—"

"Liar. Maybe it's your conscience keeping you awake."

As he stepped closer, she saw he was wearing only jeans. The sculpted muscles of his bare chest were dark and burnished in the moonlight. She shivered and looked up, but she couldn't see his features clearly—couldn't see his eyes at all.

Jessica didn't answer his accusation, but turned away from him, her teeth clenched, her hands gripping the balcony railing as she stared out over the lush, freshly watered courtyard. The scent of moisture was heavy and sweet on the night air.

It was no use. No matter how much she pretended to ignore him, her body wasn't cooperating. She was trembling from head to toe.

"What is it you want from me?" she asked in exasperation. "Do you want me to beg your forgiveness? Tell you how sorry I am for keeping Tommy a secret?"

"That would be a start, instead of running away every time I come near."

"Me?" she said. "You're the one who skipped lunch and dinner. No one knew where you were.

If you'd been in danger, we wouldn't have known where to start to look for you."

"Your concern is touching."

"All right, Diego." She sighed. "Enough. Enough of this sparring. Let's make this simple. Say whatever the hell you want to say to me and be done with it." She glared at him, but she still couldn't see into his eyes.

Somehow she thought that might be a blessing.

He walked across the landing that separated the balconies. He was so close now she could see his eyes glittering in the moonlight.

"Why, Jess? Is that simple enough for you? Just tell me why."

Jessica was trembling when she backed away from him. She'd started down the steps into the courtyard when she heard a rustle in the bushes. Then she heard an eerily familiar metallic click that made her blood run cold.

In an instant, Diego had her, pulling her back and pushing her behind him. Without thinking, she grabbed onto the arm he held back around her. His skin was warm beneath her hand and she could feel the ripple of muscles when he moved.

"Hank?" Diego called into the darkness. He held a pistol in his right hand.

"Hey, it's just me, boss. I heard voices and thought I'd best come and check. Everything OK?"

He stepped out from the shadows. In the lamplight, Jessica saw a tall, dark-haired man dressed in black. He carried what looked like an assault rifle.

"Everything's fine, Hank. Thanks."

The man nodded at them, then turned, disappearing like a ghost into the shadows of the garden.

Diego pushed the pistol into the back waistband of his jeans and then slowly turned, releasing Jessica.

"You have a man stationed outside our rooms?"

"Men," he corrected, nodding toward the darkness. "In the best of situations, they can see you, but you—or anyone else—won't ever see them."

"I'm not sure I like this." She shivered.

"Sorry, but I'm not taking any chances with . . ." He hesitated.

"With your son," she said softly, surprised at how good it felt to say those words.

"Or with you." For the first time since he had come back, his voice was devoid of bitterness. "I couldn't let anything happen to Tommy's mom, now could I?"

"I'm not sure you mean that."

Diego looked down at her for a moment as the moonlight turned her hair into a soft feathery mass of silver. She was so small, yet this spirited woman made him feel such overwhelming urges— and not just protectiveness. There was more, so much more he couldn't let himself think it. The emotions he'd thought buried and gone were as real and alive as they'd ever been.

Slowly, insidiously, and so sweetly, she had crept back into his mind.

This close, the feel of her hands on his arm still vivid, he felt himself forgetting every resentment he'd held onto so tightly. As for the vows he'd made before coming back to the McLean ranch, he couldn't seem to remember those, either.

That stubborn little look on her face, her brave words, didn't fool him. He had to admit, if only to himself, she still had the power to move him and to touch his heart. The realization of that after all this time, after what she'd done, confounded him.

"We need to talk." He no longer trusted himself to stand close to her in the moonlight.

"Not here." She nodded toward the courtyard. "I . . . I don't want to be so far away from Tommy."

Her voice faltered only slightly at the lie. What she didn't say, couldn't say, was that she didn't trust herself alone with him. Certainly not in the courtyard, where they had shared so many good times together.

"Neither do I." He took her arm, pulling her toward the French doors of his bedroom. "Tommy had a bad dream and asked if he could get in bed with me."

He pushed the doors open. A small lamp was lit and its dim glow spread over the bed, casting shadows and ridges across the form of their sleeping son.

Picking up a shirt from the bed, Diego slid his

arms into the sleeves. Jessica watched from the corner of her eyes, almost shy. It was obvious how well he took care of himself. Physically, his body was perfect. He was beautiful, and the sight of him almost took her breath away. When he turned, she saw a raised red scar on his left shoulder. Without thinking, she made a quiet sound of dismay.

Diego looked up.

"What happened?" She almost reached out to touch him.

"A bullet wound." He shrugged the shirt onto his shoulders and began buttoning it. "Nothing serious."

Jessica didn't even realize that she made another quiet murmur. But Diego noticed, and it surprised him. He could almost believe the concern in her eyes was genuine.

Jessica clenched her fist, willing herself to be still and not touch him. She had to make herself turn away.

She walked to the bed and stood for a moment looking down at Tommy. When she turned to Diego, tears glittered on her lashes, and he couldn't be certain if the tears were for him or for their son.

Diego frowned at the ache in his heart. She puzzled him. How could she pretend such concern after what she'd done?

"He's a sweet boy, Diego. Always so agreeable and easy."

Diego grunted softly. "*Unlike* his father."

She attempted a smile as she pulled a tissue

from a box near the bed. "You were raised in an entirely different atmosphere. Besides, he *is* half mine."

Even though she was making an effort at lightness, it didn't quite erase the sadness and regret in her eyes.

"Oh, yeah, right," he said, smiling only a little. "Your stubbornness and my pride. We're lucky he isn't in reform school by now."

Jessica laughed out loud, then covered her mouth and glanced at the sleeping boy.

She'd forgotten how funny Diego's self-deprecating humor could be. She stood looking at him, wanting to know all about how he was shot, needing to know how he'd felt and if he'd been alone or scared. There was so much she wanted to tell him, but she had no idea how to begin.

"Jess," he said, his eyes darkening and growing more serious. "I want my son. And I don't want another day to pass without his knowing he has a dad who cares about him." He lifted his hands in a halfhearted entreaty.

"I know, but we have to go slow. I don't want to lose him. I can't, Diego. He's my life."

"Why would you think you would lose him?" He stared at her oddly.

"I'm just so . . . so afraid of—"

"Afraid of me?" He frowned.

She didn't answer, but her eyes said it all.

"Is that what it's come to, Jess? My God, you're afraid of me?"

She had to look away from his eyes, away from

the pain she saw there. Pain she knew she had caused.

"I'm not afraid of you, but of what you might do. After what I did, some people might say you'd be justified."

"I'm not some people. You don't have to be afraid of me or of anything I do," he said, his tone blunt. "There is no way I'd want my son to be raised without his mother." He pointed toward two comfortably upholstered chairs separated by a small round table.

Despite his words, Jessica still felt uneasy . . . restless. She walked over and sank into one of the chairs.

"As long as the decisions we make are between us, and only us," he said, "then neither of us has anything to be afraid of. Agreed?" He sat on the edge of the other chair, leaning forward in a guarded manner. "There was a time when we trusted one another completely."

"I know," she whispered.

"Well?"

"I do agree," she said. "Of course I do. As long as your demands are not unreasonable."

"Me?" he asked, feigning surprise. "Unreasonable?"

She smiled, her gaze moving self-consciously away from his as she pushed her hand down the arm of the chair.

"I think I deserve an answer to my earlier question."

"You want to know why." She still didn't meet his eyes.

"Why did you keep Tommy from me?"

Jessica took a deep breath and forced herself to look at him. He was so intense, his body wound as tightly as a spring. But that intensity, that passion, was one of the things she loved about him.

One of the things she *had* loved, she corrected herself silently.

"I . . . I was hurt when you left."

"Hurt?" It wasn't that he couldn't imagine her being hurt, but it was hardly what he expected. After all, when Frank McLean had come to him offering money, he'd said Jessica wanted out of the relationship.

"You always said we were too different." She ignored his question. "I didn't realize for a long time what you meant." She paused for a moment, glancing at him. "You had a lot to prove, and there was so much resentment, so much bitterness in you. I came to realize, after a while, nothing could change that. You had to leave here in order to prove to yourself you were as good, as smart as anyone else. I'm sure the way my father treated you was responsible for a lot of that. I finally realized you couldn't stay here and still make the changes you needed in your life."

"You sound so reasonable," Diego said, his voice hard and cynical. "Too reasonable."

"You think I didn't understand?"

"How could you? You are a beautiful, wealthy woman, a princess who grew up with everything she ever wanted, with every assurance she and her world were perfect."

She looked into his eyes. "I'd like to think I've grown up a little since then."

"You knew where I was. You could have called, written. But you didn't."

"Did you think I'd beg you to come back?" she snapped. "Do you think you're the only person who has a sense of pride?"

Her mouth trembled just a little, but she managed to continue. "At first I was bitter . . . and stubborn." She smiled weakly, acknowledging his earlier assessment of her. "And then after about a year, I couldn't think how I would explain waiting so long. As the months and years went by, I guess I was just afraid." She shrugged, knowing her excuses sounded unreasonable and weak.

Diego shook his head impatiently and stood up. He paced across the room, his bare feet making no sound on the Navajo carpet. He pushed his hands through his hair, every movement reflecting frustration and impatience.

"Damn it, Jessica," he said, "this just doesn't make sense to me."

She looked up at him, frowning as she watched him pacing.

"You say you were hurt, resentful, bitter." He counted them off on his fingers, then stopped, leaning forward and staring hard at her. "Why? How could you claim to be any of those things when you were the one who wanted me gone?"

"What are you talking about?" she asked, her look puzzled.

The muscles in Diego's jaw clenched and unclenched and he took a deep breath, rolling his eyes toward the ceiling before allowing himself to continue.

"How much money did you think it would take to get me to go and never look back?" he asked, his voice hard and accusing. "Funny, I never asked what the amount was. Maybe I didn't want to know just how small a price you were willing to put on what was between us."

There was a slight stirring in the bed and Tommy sat up, rubbing his eyes and looking about the room.

"Mommy?"

"Shhh," Jessica sprang from her chair and went to the bed, hugging Tommy and coaxing him back down beneath the covers. "It's all right, baby. Go back to sleep. We didn't mean to wake you."

She glanced pointedly at Diego and he sighed, walking to the balcony doors and pushing them open. She could see his outline as the dim moonlight splashed over his hair and shoulders.

"I had a bad dream and Diego said it was all right if I got in bed with him."

"It is all right," she said, softly reassuring him. The last thing she wanted was for him to be afraid of displeasing her, and she certainly didn't want to cause him doubt or fear.

"Where is he?" he asked, his eyes opening and closing sleepily.

"He's here," she said. "Just out on the balcony."

Tommy smiled, contented, and just as quickly as he woke, he was asleep again.

Jessica walked out onto the balcony, pulling one of the doors closed behind her and leaving the other open so she could see into the room.

She went to the railing, standing away from Diego, allowing herself to study his face. She could still feel the tension in him, but for the life of her she had no idea what had set him off or what he meant about her wanting him gone, about money. "What were you accusing me of in there?"

He turned slowly to her, as if still trying to regain control. "Don't tell me you don't know. I don't believe that."

Jessica sighed. How could they be finding communication so difficult? It certainly had never been before. Or had it?

Now that she thought about it, every disagreement they ever had ended in kisses. Before they knew it, their fears and resentments were forgotten, swept aside by their passion for one another.

"We're getting nowhere this way, so I'll start." Her voice dropped lower and became a bit tentative. "You were the first man I ever loved. The only man I've ever loved." She swallowed hard.

Diego made a soft noise in his throat and she held up her hand.

"I'm sure you find it hard to believe anything I say, but let me finish."

Diego stepped back. With a quiet sigh, he nodded for her to continue.

"You always said I could never understand how you felt about your being poor, your mother being our cook and you a hired hand. I thought I could. I thought I did. But I was so young, Diego, so naive. What I didn't say to you then was that I felt so much of your resentment was mostly just male pride. I'm not saying I understand any better now, but I have learned a lot, whether you believe that or not."

Diego frowned at her, pursing his lips as if considering her words carefully, but he said nothing.

"When you finished school and came back here to the ranch, I foolishly thought—dreamed—you would work for my father, perhaps even one day become a full partner."

Diego shook his head and laughed, making a quiet noise of skepticism.

"Well, I admit I was naive. I guess I dreamed it because it was what I wanted more than anything. And when you left with hardly a word to me, without even saying you'd call or write, what was I to think? I couldn't tell you then about the baby. You can call it stubbornness if you want to, but knowing you would only stay because of your sense of obligation was not an option for me."

Diego tensed noticeably, hearing her words.

"You knew when I left you were pregnant, and you still didn't tell me?" The anger and disbelief in Diego's voice made Jessica cringe.

"Yes. I told my mother."

"And let me guess," he said, his step toward her almost menacing. "Your father knew it, too."

"No, I asked my mother not to tell him. I wanted to tell you first."

"Did you ever know your mother to keep anything from Frank McLean?" His voice was gruff and accusing.

"No," she said meekly. "I suppose not."

"All right, then," he said. "Now let me tell you my side of the story, just in case you might be telling the truth and really *don't* know what happened." He turned away from her to face the courtyard, his hand gripping the railing as if he might rip it out of its concrete base.

"I wanted to leave the ranch, that's true. But I'd intended asking you to wait for me until I was settled in Austin. I even intended to give you a ring."

Jessica gasped softly as she stared at him, trying hard to see his face in the gloom.

"But before I could talk to you, your father came to me with an offer."

"Oh, no." Why had she never guessed this? Why had it never once crossed her mind she could have been wrong about Diego's reasons for leaving? Her own insecurities had made her think no one could love her for herself alone.

"Oh, yes. He said you were too young, that our relationship was too serious and that it frightened you . . . that *I* frightened you, and you didn't know how to get out of the situation. He offered me money, Jessica, lots of money to go and never look back."

"And you believed him?"

"Of course I believed him. Why wouldn't I? A mixed-breed kid, raised without a home, in love with the daughter of one of Texas's richest, most powerful men. By all rights, I was a loser, a kid with only a slim chance of being anything other than a migrant worker like my father. Yes, I believed him!"

"But you didn't take the money." Knowing his pride, she knew the answer to that before she asked. But she had to hear him say it.

"No, I didn't take the damned money. I told your father exactly what he could do with it. But I did leave and I never wrote you, never called, tried never to look back. I thought it was what you wanted."

Jessica was speechless with shame. She had been so wrong. All this time, she had been dead wrong about everything. But the pain in her heart was for Diego and what he must have thought. Her father's actions had only reinforced the inadequacies Diego always felt about himself.

"I don't know what to say. I'm so sorry I doubted you, that my father caused all this," she whispered.

Diego rubbed his hand over his face and some of his anger seemed to dissipate.

For long moments they stood there silently, neither seeming to know how to break through the barriers that still separated them.

Diego could see Jessica's shoulders trembling. She was trying hard not to cry. Despite all the pain between them, all he wanted at this moment was to pull her into his arms and hold her.

"Go to bed, Jessica," he said heavily. "You look exhausted."

"We didn't settle anything about Tommy."

"We have plenty of time. I need to think. We both do."

Jessica looked into his shadowed eyes. She wanted to tell him all the things she was feeling, all the regrets, but most of all she wanted to hear him say he didn't hate her.

But that was impossible. There was too much pain and resentment still between them, and it didn't matter that neither was at fault. It was still there, ingrained and deep.

But there was nothing more she could say, so she crossed the landing to her own bedroom doors. She stopped and looked back once at him where he stood, still and quiet, staring out into the moonlit Texas sky.

SIX

Jessica slept very little that night. Diego's words seemed to echo again and again through her mind. Try as she might, she couldn't banish the memory of his eyes—those dark, intriguing eyes, so serious, so filled with anger and betrayal.

How much money would it have taken, he'd demanded. He'd been humiliated and hurt. Of course he had. Who wouldn't be?

Thinking back, she should have suspected her father was involved in Diego's leaving. Her father had been too quiet, too meek about Diego after that, not typical of someone whose only daughter had just been jilted, especially knowing she was pregnant. But Jessica had been in such a tailspin it had never registered in her mind.

Knowing what he'd done infuriated Jessica so much that after she left Diego, she had actually considered marching to her father's room, waking him up, and letting him know just how she felt. But she was too angry for that and she knew it. Better to wait until morning.

It was almost dawn when she finally fell into a

restless sleep. When she woke again, it was nearly nine and she'd overslept. She groaned as she glanced at the clock beside her bed.

Normally, Tommy would have been in her room long before now, coaxing her awake, snuggling beside her until she couldn't help laughing at him.

But things were different now, she reminded herself as she dragged her tired body out of bed. Tommy had Diego.

After dressing, she stood looking at herself in the mirror, as if trying to see through her eyes into her thoughts. How did she really feel about Diego's being with Tommy? After all, this was something she'd tried to avoid for years. When Diego came back, her first fear was that she would lose Tommy.

Thinking about that as she stood silent and waiting, a quiet sense of peace moved over her and she almost felt like crying.

It *was* all right. If anything, she felt a great, liberating relief that her secret was finally out in the open. Diego's being here was just as it should be, and their talk had erased any lingering resentment in her. She was no longer afraid he would take Tommy away from her. He'd said last night he would never do such a thing to her or to Tommy. And if she knew one thing about Diego, it was that he was an honorable man and would keep his word on such an important and personal matter as this.

Despite what she knew would be a long road

ahead of mending fences between them, at least this morning she felt a bit of hope.

The first mending would have to begin with her father and what he had done to Diego—what he had done to all of them.

Hurrying downstairs, she peeked into the dining room to see if Tommy was there. But the table had been cleared and the room was empty. She quickly poured herself a cup of steaming coffee from a silver carafe on the sideboard.

The door to her father's study was open slightly. He was alone. She stepped inside, and her father glanced up from his work.

Leaning back in his chair, he smiled at her. As she came closer and he saw the serious look on her face, he frowned and leaned forward as if he would come to his feet.

"Honey, what's wrong? Is it Tommy?"

"No, Dad, Tommy's fine. But something is wrong—what you did five years ago when Diego left." She stood looking down at him, her arms folded at her waist.

"So." He sighed. He stood up and turned to the windows behind his desk, standing with his hands clasped behind his back. "He told you."

"Of course he told me. Did you think he wouldn't?"

There was only the slightest shrug of her father's shoulders.

"I can't believe you did any of this. Having Diego come here without telling me—"

"If I'd told you, would you have let him come?

Would you ever have been ready to tell him about Tommy?"

"Why now, Dad?" she asked, ignoring his questions. "After all this time, after you were the one who wanted him to go in the first place—"

"I was wrong, OK?" he snapped. "Do you think I can't admit when I'm wrong? At least try to fix it? Well, I can. Maybe you don't know me as well as you think you do, girl."

Jessica took a deep breath. She was frustrated, but she could feel her anger dissipating as she looked at her father. He was right about one thing. All this couldn't be laid at his feet. She had to accept her share of the blame. So did Diego— not that she was sure that would ever happen.

But she loved her father despite his overbearing ways. Still, there were things she needed to know.

"Did you just miscalculate, having him come here to protect Tommy and me? Or did you think we were too stupid to figure out what you'd done?"

Her father did not speak, but he looked at her as if he wanted to shake her.

"For God's sake, Dad, tell me what you were thinking. Don't you think you at least owe me an explanation?"

"Girl," he said, shaking his head with exasperation, "you know yourself what I've been saying for the past two years, that it wasn't right to keep this from Diego, that he needed to know his son and Tommy needed to know his dad. But I'll admit I should have told you myself about why he left . . .

and the money." He turned and leaned back against the windowsill.

"Yes, you should have. Why didn't you?"

"I meant to. It never seemed to be the right time."

"The right time? For heaven's sake, it almost killed me when he left. You knew that. Do you have any idea how hard it was for me having Tommy alone, isolating myself out here, hiding from Diego and the rest of the world?"

"That part was not my idea." Her father shook his finger at her. "You can't blame me for that."

He lifted his chin, his eyes hardening. For a moment, Jessica glimpsed the cold, distant father she'd known as a child.

"Even in the beginning, when I had my doubts about Diego, I never asked or even encouraged you to keep the boy's existence from his own father. That, my dear, was your own decision. Your mother and I felt we had to abide by it."

Jessica moved her hand to the back of her neck, where tiny needles of tension prickled her skin and underlying muscles.

"I've had enough, Dad. As soon as this mess is over with Colby, I'm taking Tommy and leaving the ranch. I should have done it a long time ago."

"Now, Jessie, you don't mean that." He pushed himself away from the window and walked around the edge of his desk, stopping a few feet from his daughter. He might have touched her but for the warning look in her troubled eyes. "Baby, you wouldn't take my only grandchild from me," he said, his voice soft. "Don't do anything you'll regret now. Tommy's happy here. You don't want to confuse him any more than is necessary about this whole matter."

Jessica took a deep breath and shook her head. He always sounded so reasonable, so right about everything.

"Just give yourself and Diego a few days to adjust to this new situation. There's plenty of time to decide what you want to do."

"I don't have any choice about waiting. Thanks to you and the way you handled the Colby matter, I'm stuck here whether I like it or not."

"You're angry."

"Of course I'm angry. You've done it again, Dad—manipulated my life the way you always have, and I was stupid enough to let you do it. But not any more. I swear, never again."

"Is this Diego's idea? Has he asked you to leave here with him?"

Jessica's mouth fell open. "Dear Lord," she whispered. "You just don't get it, do you? Do you think Diego would have anything to do with me after what I've done? After what *you* did? Do you have any idea how much he resented your high-handed behavior toward him and his mother, not to mention your insult of offering him money to leave here? I'm surprised he hasn't already walked in here and punched you out."

Her father smiled wryly and nodded toward the doorway.

"Maybe that's exactly what he intends to do."

Jessica glanced around and saw Diego standing there, his shoulder against the doorframe. Her eyes moved quickly, hungrily over him, noting how the soft faded jeans and worn denim shirt fit his lean body. His expression gave nothing away, she thought, except for a slight impatient movement at the edge of his mouth.

As if he hadn't heard any of their conversation, Diego lifted his hand and rapped on the door.

Jessica tugged at her shirt, then turned around and plumped up a pillow in a nearby chair. Her cheeks burned with heat not only because of her anger at her father, but because Diego had probably heard everything she said, had heard her confessing her devastation at losing him.

But it wasn't only that. Just being in the same room with him, with his amazing black eyes studying her so curiously, was enough to make her blush.

"Where's Tommy?" she asked, still not meeting his eyes.

"In the kitchen with Rosie and the cook, having a snack."

"Come in, Diego. I'm afraid I'm not handling any of this very well, as Jessica was just pointing out."

As soon as Diego stepped into the room and closed the door, Frank McLean spoke.

"I owe you an apology, son, and I wouldn't blame you if you did want to take a swing at me."

Jessica had often heard that soft, cajoling tone in her father's voice. It was the way he did business, with a soft voice and a sledgehammer hidden behind his back. Most people considered it charming, but she knew it for what it was—and so, she would guess, did Diego.

"First of all, I'm not your son," Diego said, his eyes cold and hard. "And second, I don't take swings at old men."

Frank McLean laughed, a short bark of sound. But there was a slight twitch of surprise at the edge of his mouth. He shrugged his shoulders as if the shirt he wore had suddenly become uncomfortable.

"Well," Frank said, recovering quickly, "I guess I deserve that. Nevertheless, I do apologize to both of you. I'm not very good at apologies. Not very good at listening either, I guess."

"I don't know what possessed him to do such a thing." Jessica glanced at Diego, not letting her eyes meet his. She could feel his gaze on her, feel his puzzled look. But she couldn't look at him. She just couldn't.

"I thought I was doing the right thing for Jessica," Frank shrugged. "And believe it or not, I thought I was doing what was best for you, too, Diego."

When Jessica finally managed to look at Diego, she saw his eyes narrow, saw the hard set of his jaw. He wasn't buying her father's apology.

"That's the problem. You always think you're doing the right thing. But the trouble is, you never stop to consider what might be right for anyone else, not even when you're making life-changing decisions for them," she said.

"That was the old me," Frank said. "I've changed since then. That's all I can say. Your mother's death changed me, Jessie. You know that. And then when Tommy came along . . . well, I guess I saw what was really important in my life for the first time."

"That's not saying much for how you felt about your daughter, is it?" Diego asked.

"Now wait a minute—" Frank began.

"It's all right, Diego. You don't have to defend me. I've always known I wasn't the most important thing in his life." She didn't want a fight. All she wanted at the moment was for the conversation to end. "He had changed—or I thought he had until he pulled this latest stunt, bringing you here without telling me, forcing me to tell you about Tommy in a way that wasn't good for either of us."

Again she glanced at Diego. He was still watching her, and his expression had hardly softened. "Not that I'm any less guilty than he is. I couldn't blame you if you hated us all."

Diego said nothing.

"Don't you have anything to say?" she asked finally.

"What do you expect me to say?" Diego looked formidable today, his shirt sleeves rolled up to reveal strong tanned arms, the holster he wore emphasizing his broad muscular shoulders. With his chin up, he looked through narrowed eyes at her.

"That all is forgiven? That an apology can make up for the years I missed with my son? Maybe the honor of living in your house and eating at your table is supposed to fix everything."

Jessica bit her lower lip as she glanced first at Diego, then at her father. Frank McLean wasn't used to standing by quietly and letting someone rip into him. The sight of his doing just that, even doing it meekly, was a shock.

"Personally, I'd just as soon we don't mention any of it again. But I will say this." Diego addressed Frank. "Regardless of everything that's happened in the past, the future with Tommy belongs to us. Whatever happens with our son is a decision between Jessie and me, Mr. McLean. It won't be based on money or power or your convenience, but on what's best for Tommy. If you interfere in any way, I might consider taking Jessica's suggestion about punching you out. Do I make myself clear?"

Diego's dark eyes glittered dangerously, and Jessica felt a shiver race over her. She couldn't blame him for still harboring all the resentments he'd ever had. As far as he was concerned, nothing had changed for him here. He was still the outsider.

"I understand you perfectly," Frank McLean said, his voice quiet and solemn. He started to step forward, as if he might offer his hand. Then, seeing Diego's eyes, he stopped, rubbing his hand first against his pants, then self-consciously pushing it down into his pocket.

"I have work to do," Diego said, turning. His

gaze caught Jessica's. "The sooner we get this done, the sooner I can get out of here."

Jessica opened her mouth to speak. She'd thought . . . hoped . . . that now this was all out in the open, they could talk about Tommy, even resolve their past. But before she could say a word, he had walked out the door.

Jessica started after him.

"Let him go, Jessica," her father said. "Let him cool off a little."

"No, Dad, I've waited long enough. I want this settled and done with."

She hurried out of the study. By the time she caught up with Diego, he was at work on the front veranda. There were wires everywhere and boxes of surveillance equipment sat on the tiles.

"I have work to do, Jess."

"We have to talk. I have to know what you intend to do about Tommy."

He glanced up from what he was doing and one brow arched upward.

"I haven't decided yet. You've waited four years," he said sarcastically. "What's the big hurry now?"

"Well, when are you going to decide? I can't stand this."

"Don't push this, Jessica. Not now. Not here."

"Damn you." Anger sparked in her green eyes. She hated this coolness in him. She was prepared to accept any terms he wanted with his son, but did he have to be so damned cold toward her? "I don't understand why you're acting this way."

"You don't," he said, his voice flat.

"No, damn it, I don't. I thought last night after we talked, after you realized I didn't know about Dad's offer, that—"

"That what, Jess? That I would thank you for telling me now, when you were forced to?"

"Oh," she said, stung by his words.

"Just let it rest, Jessica." He turned away as if he would go back to work.

She wanted a response from him, wanted to see some spark in him, something she could grasp onto and deal with. She didn't know how to fight this hard, distant coldness.

"You're just so cool, aren't you?" she said, her voice rough with hidden tears. "So unmoved by anything or anyone."

With a low growl, he threw down the wires he was working on and in one quick movement his hands came forward to grasp her shoulders, pushing her back into the shade of the veranda.

"What do you want from me, Jess?" he whispered, his voice hard and angry. "Tell me. Or do you even know?"

She couldn't move, couldn't breathe, couldn't speak. All she could think about was his eyes, his mouth, the hard touch of his hands, and the way his body felt against hers.

"I . . . I don't know. I—"

"If I'm cool, it's because I had to learn to be. And as far as being moved . . ." His hand moved up her arm and along her shoulder to her neck. He touched her face, his thumb trailing down to the corner of her mouth. "Believe me, Jess, if it makes you feel any better, you still have the power to move me. Is that what you want to hear?"

"Yes," she whispered. "It is Diego. I still want—"

"I can't trust you," he whispered, shaking his head against her softly spoken entreaty. "Damn it, I can't."

"You can." She wasn't thinking, only reacting to his nearness when she lifted her mouth to his, her eyes searching every inch of his beautiful, sensuous face.

He stepped away from her, letting the air escape slowly from his lungs. "The past is gone and we can never go back. But you're the one who changed everything, Jess. Not me."

"Diego . . ." she said, trying one last time to get through to him.

"Look, I can't do this. It's no good for either of us. While I'm here, just pretend I'm someone you never knew. Think of me as a stranger, a law officer with no emotional ties, sent here to do a job. It will be better for all of us that way."

Quickly he turned away from her, kicking at the wires and boxes as he walked off the veranda and across the yard toward the barn.

Her fingers moved to touch her trembling lips and she could feel her tears starting to fall.

"Pretend I never knew you?" she whispered. "Oh, Diego, I'm not so sure I can do that. I'm not sure about anything anymore."

SEVEN

That night Diego paced the floor of his room. No matter how disciplined he knew himself to be, no matter how hard he tried, he couldn't seem to banish the image of Jessica's face from his mind.

Today, looking into her expressive green eyes, he'd been surprised to see such sadness and conflict—even genuine regret, if he'd let himself believe it. He was surprised how much her sadness affected him.

"Hell," he muttered.

Why should it bother him? What did she expect?

He might believe she had nothing to do with Frank McLean's offer of money five years ago, but she had kept his son's existence from him. When he asked himself why she'd done such a thing, he could only come up with the same old reason: He wasn't good enough for the McLean family, never had been, never would be.

Had he thought by coming back here he could change that?

Walking across the room, he stood at the French doors, gazing out over the moonlit courtyard. So little had changed he sometimes felt as if he'd never left. He couldn't help remembering the nights he'd spent with Jess here. In fact, he constantly had to fight back memories. There were reminders of her and of those times everywhere he looked. And now he had another reminder. Tommy.

Despite knowing the cold, hard facts about what Jessica had done, that hot, quick, invisible thread of passion was still there between them, as strong as ever. And nothing, not distance, not even time, had broken its hold.

He cursed under his breath and shook his head.

From a distant, hidden rafter came the low coo of a dove. A red flicker of light caught at the corner of his vision, pulling his gaze up to where a jet moved across the night sky.

So many nights like this they had lain together on a blanket, staring up at the Texas sky, watching the moon and the stars. For hours, they would watch jets sail across the heavens, guessing where they were going and who was aboard. They'd imagine themselves inside, flying away on some great adventure. Then they'd laugh and kiss and make love again, hating to say good night, hating to be apart for the few hours left until dawn.

Diego watched until the jet was out of sight before moving back into the darkened room. Then he sighed heavily and walked to a chair near the doorway that led to Jessica's room.

Sitting in the chair, his legs sprawled in front of him, he rubbed his unshaven jaw and stared mutely at the closed door. It was unlocked as always, he knew.

His mind immediately pictured her room . . . her bed. The thought of her lying there wouldn't go away—her hair tumbled against the pillow, her lips parted in sleep. She was so close, so warm, he could almost feel her.

"Hellfire," he muttered. He stood up quickly and moved away from the door.

He should hate her for what she'd done.

Yet he was still drawn to her as if there had been no years separating them, as if she had not rejected him in the worst possible way a woman could reject a man—by withholding his child.

His mind might understand that part, might even believe she was genuinely sorry. But he couldn't explain these other feelings he was having. Somewhere deep inside, in a place he thought he'd buried long ago, he still wanted her, and his body couldn't seem to distinguish the irony in that knowledge.

Like a magnet, the door pulled his gaze toward it again. It would be so easy to walk through that door to her bed. What would she do, he wondered, if he came to her, slid into bed beside her?

Diego swallowed hard. His suppressed thoughts could no longer be held at bay. The memories were so real, and now that he was here again, they rushed in, tearing at him like a dangerous riptide.

He closed his eyes and leaned his head back.

She would welcome him. He'd seen that much

in her eyes today. He knew it as surely as he breathed.

Slowly, sweetly, she would turn to him, snuggle warmly against him. She might utter a soft little sound of surprise, but she would open her arms to him, wrap her long, beautiful legs around him . . .

"God," he rasped. He stood up quickly and moved further away from the door and the temptation it hid.

His boss back in Austin had asked Diego if he could handle this assignment. When Diego had said yes, he'd been so certain. Now he wasn't certain of anything.

How had he managed to convince himself that living here in the same house with Jessica would be possible, that being near her wouldn't be a temptation every minute of every day?

He shook his head and poured a drink of water from a nearby pitcher.

He'd taken the assignment, convinced no other Ranger could protect Jessica the way he could. And now he was protecting his son. He had no other choice. He couldn't escape the assignment now—or the temptation.

But did he really want to escape? Had something in the back of his subconscious wanted to come here again? Wanted to see her again, touch her, make love to her?

If that were the case, the joke was on him. He never dreamed in a million years that Jess would betray him or that he'd come here and find a son he never knew existed. The Jessica he knew never could have done such a thing.

Diego shook his head, trying to banish the thoughts and images.

It was late. If he expected to be of any use tomorrow, he had to get to sleep. A lot of work needed to be done before the papers could be served on Colby, and the longer the delay, the better the chance Colby's impending arrest might be leaked.

Diego couldn't let that happen.

He would sleep. He'd make himself. It was simply a question of mind over matter, one of a number of necessary disciplines he'd learned over the years.

Once in bed, he lay breathing slowly and evenly, trying to stop his mind's emotional battering of visions and memories.

The fact was, he and Jessica had loved one another and between them they'd made a sweet, handsome little boy. Even now, just thinking about him, Diego's heart turned over with love and pride.

He'd been taken by surprise by this new sense of love and fierce protectiveness he felt. He'd never imagined how deeply a father could be connected to a child.

He couldn't blame Jessica for what her father had done, but she was the one responsible for keeping Tommy from him. How could he *not* blame her for that?

But could he forgive her, knowing she'd been

young, overwhelmed by a first, passionate love, as he had been? If she honestly thought he'd left because he didn't love her, didn't want to commit to her, of course she'd be bitter and scared. Even vengeful.

He let the air out of his lungs in a soft whoosh.

All right, he'd give her that.

But how in hell could he let himself trust her again, take the chance on her ripping out his heart as she had with Tommy?

Disciplined or not, it was almost dawn before he finally closed his eyes.

For the next few days, Diego managed to avoid Jessica except at mealtime, and sometimes even then. He worked hard and went to his room at night exhausted.

When he could, he rode. Sometimes he took Tommy with him. But no matter where he was or what he did, when he returned to the house, when he saw Jessica, he often felt her troubled gaze following him. He saw the questions in her eyes, but there was nothing he could say—not until he worked through all this in his own way.

One night, despite working himself into a state of exhaustion, Diego was having another bout of sleeplessness.

He heard a sound from Tommy's room and went to stand in the doorway between their rooms.

The little boy seemed restless, but after a few seconds, he quieted.

Diego went back to bed and had just closed his eyes when he felt someone's presence beside him.

He sat up in bed. "Tommy?" he asked. "What's wrong, son? Did you have a bad dream?"

"I don't feel good."

Diego swung his legs around, his feet coming to rest on the floor. He reached for Tommy and felt the heat emanating from his small body before he ever touched his skin.

"You're burning up," he murmured. "Do you feel sick? Does your tummy hurt?"

"No." Tommy's voice sounded hoarse. "My throat hurts. And my head hurts. Can I get in bed with you?"

"Sure you can, sport," Diego replied, his voice soft with tenderness and a patience he never knew he possessed. He stood up and settled Tommy into bed, pulling the sheets up, only to have Tommy kick them away.

"Hot."

"I'm going to get your mom," Diego said. "You be real still, OK?"

Tommy nodded, his eyes closed. He looked so small, so pale and helpless lying there alone in the big bed.

Diego pulled on a pair of jeans, fastening them hurriedly as he moved across the room. His heart was pounding as wildly as if he were in a hostage situation or a shoot-out.

As soon as he entered Jessica's room, she sat up in bed as if she'd been expecting him. But it was only a mother's instinct, Diego knew. He was certain she'd been sleeping soundly.

"What's wrong?" she asked, her voice soft and sleepy.

Before he could answer, she was out of bed, pulling her arms into a robe that lay on the foot of her bed.

"It's Tommy," Diego said. "He's not feeling well."

Jessica rushed past him and through the doorway. The light material of her robe billowed out behind her like a cloud, leaving a faint sweet, exotic scent in her wake.

She sat on the edge of the bed, touching Tommy's forehead and his face, then running her hands down over his arms and hands.

He stirred and opened his eyes.

"Honey, where does it hurt? You got that old sore throat again?"

"He's burning up," Diego said. He towered above Jessica, first leaning toward her, then moving away, his movements restless and impatient.

Tommy placed his hand on his throat and swallowed, his eyes imploring and a little frightened.

Jessica reached behind her, toward Diego.

"There should be a flashlight over there in the top drawer."

Diego found the light and handed it to Jessica, then watched as she placed her fingers under Tommy's chin.

"Open up, baby. Let Mommy look at your throat."

Diego was amazed at her patience and her calmness. His own insides were churning. He needed to do something, anything. Standing by and watching someone else take charge of a situation was not his strong point, but he'd never felt more helpless or more out of his element.

"Hmmm." Jessica turned off the flashlight and brushed Tommy's hair away from his forehead.

"What?" Diego asked. "For God's sake, Jess . . ."

Jessica stood up and faced him, frowning and putting her finger to her lips. Until now she hadn't really noticed how agitated he was, hadn't seen the worried lines across his brow.

She realized with a jolt of surprise that he was frightened. This strong, independent man who faced danger every day, who matched wits with dangerous men and dangerous situations for a living, actually had fear in his eyes because his little boy had a fever.

"He's OK," she whispered, her voice sweet and patient. "Just a little sore throat."

"How do you know? How can you be sure it isn't something more serious?"

Jessica's gaze moved over his bare chest and shoulders and down to the waistband of his jeans, where the top button was unfastened. She had to force herself to look away. Sometimes just looking at him made her lose all reason and forget whatever she meant to say.

"His throat is a little red, but I didn't see any spots or blotches. It's probably just a cold. The doctor thinks he might have some mild allergies, but so far it's never been anything serious. He says he might even outgrow it. I have some allergy medication that I keep on hand. If you'll stay with him, I'll go get it."

"How do you know all this?" Diego shook his head in wonder.

"It kind of comes gradually, I guess." She looked into his troubled eyes.

"I felt completely helpless. Panicked almost, like a school kid." His admission came easily, with no attempt to hide his emotions. For some reason that put Jessica at ease, more than anything since he had come.

"A lot of times I've felt the same way," she confessed. "But you'll learn in time, the way I did."

Diego walked to one of the chairs and sank down into it, resting his elbows on his knees. He held his hands out in front of him. "I'm shaking. Will you look at that? For God's sake, I'm shaking like a rookie."

For that brief moment, as Diego stared at his hands, Jessica watched him, her face unguarded and filled with all the tenderness she still felt and had to keep hidden. She wanted nothing more than to take him in her arms, to hold him and kiss him and tell him again how sorry she was for all she'd done. It was her fault he had never learned about childhood illnesses along with her, her fault this was all so new and troubling. The guilt of that ate at her night and day.

"I'll go get his medicine." She hurried from the room.

Going into her bathroom, she closed the door and, for a moment, leaned back against the cool wood panel. Trembling, she tried to blink away hot tears.

She had been so wrong. Because of her bitterness and stubbornness, she had robbed Diego of these simple precious moments, and in doing so she had robbed her own son of a father who loved him.

How could she expect him to forgive her for that?

EIGHT

Even though Tommy was better, Jessica decided to stay with him the next day. That night, Diego insisted on sitting with him.

"Perhaps one of your men can take over for you on the security work tomorrow."

"Why?" Diego frowned.

He always seemed so defensive. Why did he have to be so defensive?

"If you stay up all night with Tommy . . . never mind," she said, seeing the look on his face.

"Staying awake all night and working the next day is nothing new to me." His voice was cold.

"Sometimes I forget you're a big tough Texas Ranger, trained for adversity."

At her sarcasm he smiled grimly, but remained silent.

"Besides, I don't mind sitting with him again," Jessica said. "He's much better, and he'll probably sleep through the night anyway. Rosie can help if I need her."

"I *want* to do it, OK?" Diego's look was so fierce that Jessica didn't question him again.

"Fine," she said. "Wake me if you need any-thing."

Later that evening, she stood in the shadows of her room just behind the doorway, watching Diego read to Tommy. She liked it best when Diego didn't know she was there.

She felt someone beside her and turned to find Rosie at her side.

"That man has fallen head over heels in love with his boy, hasn't he?" Rosie whispered.

Jessica glanced at Rosie, observing the soft, ap-proving look on her face.

"I'm sure you and everyone else in this house think I've done him a great disservice by keeping Tommy's existence from him."

"I didn't say that."

"You don't have to. It's all over your face. The others, too."

Rosie shrugged, not denying Jessica's words. "He's a good man," Rosie said. "We all liked him when he was here before and we like him even more now."

"A good man who didn't deserve to be shut out of his son's life."

"Are you asking what I think?" Rosie raised her brows.

"Yes, Rosie." Jessica sighed. "I guess I am."

"Well, if you want to hear me say it out loud, then, yes, I think you and your daddy were wrong. And if, standing here, watching those two together, you don't understand that, then—"

"I *do* understand," Jessica said. "That's just the

problem. I understand. I know I was wrong and I
regret what I did. But he doesn't believe me, nor
does he trust me. I don't know how to fix it, Rosie.
He's shutting me out."

"Can you blame him? It's only natural he
would." Rosie glanced at Jessica, who was biting
her lip as she watched the scene in the other bedroom.

"The past can't be fixed," Rosie said, her words
slow and thoughtful. "It just has to be endured
sometimes. But since you're asking, I'll say this—
just take a look at that man, Jessica. Most women
would give their eyeteeth for a man like him,
strong and honorable, a man who would protect
what's his with his dying breath. And yet with that
boy he's as tender and devoted as any mother
could be. Far as I'm concerned, that's the measure
of a man. Guess you know that. Guess that's why
you have that look in your eyes every time he's
around."

Jessica's first impulse was to deny it, but, seeing
the look on Rosie's face, she didn't bother. This
woman, who was like a second mother to her, had
known her too long for pretenses.

"What do I do now?"

"Well, when you ride into a box canyon, sometimes the only way out is to backtrack and start
all over."

Jessica's mouth twitched to one side at Rosie's
homespun advice. She shook her head affectionately, her laughter soft and quiet.

Rosie pulled at Jessica's sleeve before she left.

"One more thing," she said. "Just make sure when you get out, you don't turn around and go right back into that same canyon." Rosie stared straight into Jessica's eyes. "You get my meaning?"

"Oh, yes," Jessica replied, still smiling. "I get your meaning, loud and clear."

"If you need me to help, just call me." Rosie waved over her shoulder.

Diego was dreaming. He had fallen asleep with the book in his hand.

The dream was misty and warm and he couldn't see the woman on the horse very clearly. He was aware of blond hair flying in the wind and long, slender legs clutched tightly against the horse's belly as the rider bent forward, urging her mount onward.

He could hear her laughter, clear and sweet, ringing on the air.

He wanted to catch her. Every beat of his heart, every instinct in his taut body urged him to catch her. He had to see her and touch her, had to know who she was.

He moved his feet restlessly and the book fell to the floor with a soft thud. Still, he didn't waken from the dream.

Hearing a noise, Jessica got out of bed and walked softly to the open doorway. The faint glow of the lamp fell across the bed, showing the peaceful, sleeping face of her son. Diego still sat in the chair, his head bent, his chin on his chest. The book he'd been reading lay on the floor at his feet.

She smiled. Without bothering to get her robe, she tiptoed into the room, going to the bed and bending to pick up the book. Pulling a soft shawl from the foot of the bed, she stepped toward Diego and placed it carefully across him.

He still wore his shoulder holster, and it looked uncomfortable to Jessica. She couldn't remove it, but maybe she could straighten it a little.

Diego's hand came forward like a shot, grasping her wrist and pulling her toward him. His eyes were open, yet he seemed dazed and a little confused, as if he were sleepwalking.

"Don't you know better than to sneak up on someone like that?" he muttered. After he was more awake and realized who she was, he loosened his grip, but he didn't let go.

"I'm sorry," she said, her voice so soft it was almost nonexistent. "You dropped the book and I . . ."

His thumb moved against the sensitive skin just inside her wrist, exploring, caressing. She couldn't seem to say another word.

Diego's gaze darkened as it moved over her bare shoulders and half-covered breasts. Her sweet scent moved toward him like a velvet glove, encompassing him, warming him.

Neither of them spoke as they remained locked in place, unable to move away from each other.

"Why . . . why don't you carry Tommy to his own bed?" She knew how trivial her words must sound, but she needed to move past the heavy emotions that hung in the air between them. "You look tired. You probably need some rest."

"Rest is the last thing I'm thinking about right now." He looked into her eyes, studying her face and knowing he'd found the woman who had raced across his dreams only moments ago.

The look in his eyes made Jessica catch her breath. Every barrier she'd erected against him came down in that instant, and she knew he could see it on her face.

But she didn't care. All she knew was how he made her feel. How he made her want.

But what did *he* want? Was it fatigue and lack of sleep that made him act so strangely, so out of character from the way he'd been the last few days?

"Is your bed warm?" he asked, his voice rough and provocative. He tugged gently on her arm, bringing her closer until she was on her knees beside him, her hand resting against his thigh.

"Diego . . ."

"What?" He pulled her closer. "What do you want, Jess? Better say it now. For at this moment, I'm not sure I could refuse you anything."

She wasn't sure who moved first, but suddenly she was in his arms, his mouth hard against hers, bruising and sweet, his arms crushing her against him. His fingers were in her hair, pulling strands of it toward them until it covered her face and his, until its sweet, clean scent mingled with their kiss and their soft, urgent breathing.

He was aggressive and masculine. She'd always loved that about him. And now, after the past few days of anger and retreating, he had become the hunter and she the hunted.

When she pulled away and looked into his eyes, they were as black as stone. But they were no longer cold, no longer threatening.

"We . . . we can't do this," she managed, her voice shaky.

He pulled her to him again. "Why can't we? It's what we both want, isn't it? Or are you going to deny that?"

Jessica closed her eyes and swallowed hard as he kissed her again, this time softer, longer, until she was gasping for air and sanity, until her legs trembled so badly she knew she wouldn't be able to stand.

"How can I deny it?" she whispered finally.

With the last ounce of strength and willpower she had, she pulled back. Still on the floor, she scooted far enough away from those hands and that mouth so that she could think straight.

But his dark gaze followed her, refusing to let her retreat from him completely or from what she knew in her heart she wanted. His eyes questioned and accused.

"You've been so angry with me. You've hardly said a word to me for days." She wanted to explain, needed to explain. "You said you would never trust me again. And now . . ." She waved her hands ineffectually toward him, her voice faltering, her breath short. "Now you expect me to just . . . just . . ."

"Let me make love to you, Jessica." He slid out of the chair and moved beside her on the floor. "That's what I want—and I know it's what you want, too."

Jessica gasped. Her head was spinning, and she thought she'd never been so confused in all her life.

This might be the new beginning Rosie had spoken about earlier, but it might also lead right back into her metaphorical box canyon.

If she were to have a second chance—if that was what his actions meant—Jessica wanted it to be right this time. Although the physical need was there for both of them, she knew that this time she needed more than that.

She put her hand on his arm and saw the spark in his smoldering eyes.

"It's too soon," she whispered. "I . . . I'm not sure this is the right time . . . for either of us."

"Any time's the right time."

"No. You know what I mean."

He leaned away from her slightly, his eyes narrowed as he watched her. "No, I don't. Why don't you tell me exactly what you mean?"

She took a deep breath. This was so new for them, and their emotions were both still so raw from the past few days of battle.

"Sex with you"—she looked at his mouth and swallowed hard—"would be so easy—"

"And so right."

"Maybe. And maybe not."

Diego sighed heavily and moved toward her impatiently. He was tired of waiting. Tired of arguing.

Jessica placed her hand on his chest, holding him away.

"That's the problem, Diego. We never talked. We never really knew each other. If we had, I never would have assumed you'd just up and leave me, and you never would have assumed I'd ask my father to pay you off."

Diego frowned, and the muscle in his jaw tightened. "I knew you better than I've ever known anyone."

"Oh?" she asked, her smile soft and tremulous. "What's my favorite color? My favorite place?"

"Blue. And the cottonwoods by the creek, where we first made love."

Jessica knew he was deliberately provoking her. But her breath caught and her eyelashes lowered softly, then lifted again so she could stare into his eyes.

"One out of two," she whispered.

"Green," he guessed again, "like your eyes."

"Green *is* my favorite color, but guessing doesn't count."

"What do you want, Jess?" He leaned forward, his mouth nuzzling her ear. "What do you want me to say?"

"How can you have forgiven me for what I did?"

Her question seemed to take him by surprise.

He pulled away from her, frowning and studying her face for long, silent moments.

"I didn't say I had."

Jessica rolled her eyes toward the ceiling and quickly came to her feet.

"That's exactly what I mean, Diego."

"What?" He was standing now, too, his hands on his hips as he confronted her. "Is this some kind of emotional blackmail? I say I forgive you, and then you'll—"

"If I were a man, I'd deck you for that remark." Her cheeks flamed scarlet with anger.

"OK, I was out of line."

"You know exactly what I mean," she said. "How can we be . . . intimate . . . when you still have all this resentment inside you?"

He took a long breath and pursed his lips.

"Believe me, it would be easy."

"I . . . I didn't expect this."

"Bull, Jessica." His laughter was soft, disdainful. "You knew it. Hell, we both knew it the minute I first stepped into that room the other day."

"It's not that easy for a woman," she said, grasping at straws. "There needs to be more trust and friendship. We're a long way from that yet."

Diego glowered at her. "Women," he muttered, rubbing his hand against his day-old beard. "You want to talk everything to death."

"You are such a chauvinist."

"And you are too sexy for words. Jess," he growled, obviously frustrated, "I swear, if you don't get out of this room right this minute, I'm not going to be responsible for my actions."

"Yes, you will." She smiled tenderly at him. "Texas Rangers are honorable men." Her eyes darkened and her features grew serious. "Seriously, Diego, can't we call a truce till we can work through this?"

He looked at her through half-closed lids, then slowly turned and went back to the chair beside the bed. He settled in, propping his feet against the bed.

"OK, you win. A Texas Ranger always knows when to retreat."

Jessica left the room quickly, before she could change her mind—before her traitorous body pointed her toward him instead of the door.

Diego heard the door close, and he muttered softly beneath his breath.

The truth was, he'd let her win, agreed to a truce because he couldn't trust himself with her one more second. The sight of her in that gown, her hair tumbling about her face, those beautiful green eyes looking at him with such sweet pleading—hell, Texas Ranger or not, he wasn't so sure about the honorable part of him. Not tonight.

"Damn," he said, closing his eyes.

NINE

The next morning, Jessica was surprised to find Tommy's and Diego's bedrooms empty.

She found them having breakfast, with Tommy chattering away in obvious excitement.

Jessica smiled, thinking how amazing it was that children could bounce back from an illness so quickly.

Diego glanced up at her, his look wary, but she thought his anger was not as near the surface as it had been, nor did his expression hint at what had happened between them the night before.

"Mom," Tommy said, swallowing his food quickly, unable to contain his enthusiasm, "Diego's going to take me outside when we finish breakfast. He said we can go see the new colt. We're going to decide on a name today. Grandpa says we can."

"Are you sure you're feeling up to that?" She went to him and placed her hand against his face.

"Sure," he said, going back to his breakfast.

Jessica looked across at Diego and they both smiled.

It was good to see him smile. For a moment,

she could almost believe he'd never left, that there
had been no problems between them.

She had to remind herself to go slowly. *Start over,*
she told herself. *And don't fall back into that same
trap of moving too quickly.*

She poured herself a cup of coffee. "That will
be great. I have plenty to keep me occupied today." She bent and kissed Tommy, then picked up
a croissant and headed toward the door. "I'll be
in my office when you get back." She allowed her
glance to fall only briefly on Diego.

"I'll bring him in to see you before he takes his
nap."

"Nap?" Tommy complained.

"Yes, nap." Diego and Jessica spoke at the same
time, then laughed. "Now if you don't stop talking
and finish your breakfast, we're never going to get
out of here," Diego added.

Jessica smiled and shook her head when Tommy
began eating with a purpose.

For the next few days, Jessica barely saw Diego
except at mealtimes. Often he would take his
lunch with him. Sometimes he took Tommy with
him.

On those days, Tommy would be full of excitement at supper, telling Jessica and his grandfather
about what to him was some great adventure.

One evening, as Tommy talked on and on, Jessica glanced at Diego. When their eyes met, they
found themselves smiling at their son's enthusiasm.

She didn't know why it should surprise her to
see the pride in Diego's beautiful black eyes, but

it did. Her face softened and she looked down at her plate, hoping he wouldn't see her tears.

How many times she'd wished for someone to share such moments with, and now it had come true, even if it was only temporary.

It felt unbelievably right. And good.

Every time she glanced at Diego, she found him watching her, as if he had something to say.

Tommy was still talking, and now he coughed and swallowed.

"Diego and me went down—"

"Don't talk with your mouth full," Jessica cautioned.

He chewed quickly for a few moments and began to chatter again, his eyes wide and bright with excitement.

". . . we went down to the creek, where the cottonwoods grow," he said, hardly missing a beat.

Jessica looked at Diego and realized she was holding her breath.

It was their place, the place where they'd first made love. The place, no doubt, where Tommy had been conceived.

Diego coolly pulled his gaze away, concentrating on the food before him.

"I've always loved that place." Jessica didn't know what else to say.

"Can we go back tomorrow?" Tommy asked.

"Well . . . I . . ."

"Maybe your mom would like to come along this time," Diego suggested. To Jessica he added, "The fences are done and the security cameras are in place. After tomorrow, we probably won't be able to wander about the ranch at will. Better take advantage of the moment."

"Would you, Mom?"

"If Diego doesn't mind." She looked at Diego.

"I suggested it, didn't I?" His voice was cool and mysterious.

"Then of course. I'd love to go."

"Eat your dinner, son," Frank McLean said. "You're going to get indigestion. Diego, does this mean Colby will be brought in now?"

"Yes. I talked to headquarters today. The papers are ready as soon as we do one last check and give them the go-ahead. They'll probably prefer arresting him tonight, in the middle of the night—catch him off guard if they can."

Frank McLean rose to leave the table. "Then if you all will excuse me, I have some calls to make now that we know when this is going to happen." He stopped at Diego's chair. "You feel confident about this? Everything's going to work?"

"Nothing or no one will get past security unless we see it on camera first."

"Good." Frank touched Diego lightly on the shoulder. "You do good work, son. I want you to know how much it means to me."

As her father left the room, Jessica watched Diego from the corner of her eye.

His jaw tightened slightly. Then, as if to himself, he smiled and gave a quiet little laugh.

It was good, the three of them alone, finishing

their dinner, talking. For a moment Jessica let herself imagine they were a real family.

Later Rosie stepped into the room. "Would you like coffee? We have peach cobbler for dessert."

Jessica nodded.

"Sounds good," Diego said.

"Peaches." Tommy twisted his mouth to one side. "Yuck."

"Well, since you don't want dessert, buddy, how about letting Rosie take you to your room while your mom and I stay here and talk?"

Jessica frowned curiously at him. Then her heart began to beat quickly. Something was on his mind; she'd felt it all evening.

"Is something wrong?" she asked as soon as Rosie and Tommy were gone.

"No, not at all." But his face was serious and he was hesitant and thoughtful, as if choosing his words carefully. "Tommy asked me about his dad today."

Jessica made a soft murmur as she studied his face. Had it hurt him? Pleased him? His face was so emotionless she couldn't tell.

"What did you tell him?"

"Hell, I didn't know what to say." He leaned back in his chair, his forearm against the table as his fingers fiddled with a butter knife. "I'd thought if he ever asked, I'd be more than ready to tell him. But then, seeing his face, those big eyes watching me, trusting me . . . I wasn't sure how I should say it." He looked up, meeting Jessica's gaze.

Jessica's breath caught in her throat at the vulnerability in his eyes.

"So you didn't tell him anything?"

"I thought you and I . . . I thought maybe it would be best if we—"

"Tell him together?" Jessica's eyes widened and she could hardly hide her pleasure.

"Yeah, maybe."

"Oh, Diego." She bit her lip to stop its trembling. She'd been more emotional these past few days than she'd ever been in her life. Diego probably thought that she was a complete mental case. "Thank you," she managed. "That means so much to me."

He seemed a bit stunned at her words.

"It's only right," he said. "You are his mother."

"After what I did, I'm surprised you think I have any rights at all."

"I do." His face was serious and thoughtful. "Besides, I'm trying to do what's right for Tommy."

"I think having the best interest of a child at heart is the true measure of a good parent, and that's my biggest regret about all this." Her voice dropped. "I know I didn't do what was best for him."

"Look, Jessica, I don't think you need to have any regrets about Tommy. He's a fine boy, well adjusted and happy."

"You think so?"

"I think so," he answered.

The emotions rising inside of her were a surprise. She wanted to hug him, wanted to snuggle her face against the side of his neck and just breathe. She wanted to look into his eyes and see pleasure and admiration, wanted to see his mouth reaching for hers. She wanted so many things she could hardly name them all.

"So." She needed to change the subject. "The trip to the cottonwoods, the three of us. Is that really OK with you?"

"Sure, if it's OK with you—if it isn't too soon. I don't want you to think I'm trying to put you in a difficult situation . . . you know, telling him there, in a place with a lot of memories . . . for both of us. He just seems to enjoy it so much."

"I understand. It's fine. Really."

"Good. Tomorrow at noon, then? We'll take a picnic."

"Tommy will love it," she whispered.

The next day was hot, with a dry wind blowing across the Texas plains. Small dust clouds swirled along the ground like miniature tornadoes, but overhead the sky was a brilliant clear blue, with not a cloud anywhere.

Jessica dressed for the weather, wearing comfortable jeans and boots and a light cotton shirt.

Tommy was so excited he could hardly contain himself. While Jessica dressed, he ran from her room to his, wondering if he should take a favorite toy, asking finally if he could take a toy pistol with him on the picnic.

"Honey, there's no sense taking stuff out there

that we're just going to have to carry back. Take
one thing, OK? Just one." She grinned as he ran
back through Diego's room to his own and came
back with a small leather holster and shiny water
pistol.

She laughed and shook her head, wondering if
she should be worried about this sudden interest
in guns and manly pursuits. She was sure it was
merely the result of being with Diego and seeing
him carry a gun. He had become Tommy's hero
in such a short time.

They met Diego in the paddock near the barn.
The horses were already saddled and the leather
saddlebags across Diego's mount bulged with picnic supplies.

When Diego looked up and saw them, his eyes
moved quickly over Jessica.

"Morning." Diego forced himself to pull his
gaze away from her. He laughed aloud when
Tommy came racing toward him, his short sturdy
legs churning. A small leather holster flapped
against his hip as he ran.

"What's this, cowboy?" Diego asked, bending
and lifting the holster at Tommy's side, then letting it fall. He glanced up again as Jessica came
to stand with them. "Is this our bodyguard today?"

"I think so," she replied, unable to keep herself
from returning his smile. "And Mom is a little
concerned about his sudden obsession with guns,"
she added more quietly.

Diego gave her a look of surprise, then nodded.

"I'll talk to him about it, if it'll make you feel better."

"It would."

She loved it when Diego was like this. His greeting was slow and unhurried, the look in his eyes warm and welcoming. Most of all, she loved the way he was with Tommy. It delighted her to see how much he obviously cared for her son.

Our son, she corrected, reminding herself of the reason for this trip.

For a moment, a chill rippled up her spine and she couldn't repress a shiver. Today would change her life forever.

"You all right?" Diego asked. "Want a jacket or sweater?"

He never missed a thing, she thought. Perhaps it was his Ranger training. Sometimes it was downright eerie how he picked up on the smallest gesture, the most fleeting of looks.

"In this weather?" She hoped to feign cool indifference. She wasn't sure it worked. "No, I'm fine," she added, stepping to her horse and hooking a small bag to the saddle horn.

As they rode out from the paddock and onto a dirt road leading away from the house, Jessica deliberately let her gaze wander, taking in the distant purplish mountains and smiling at the other horses that ran along the fenceline with them, as if they longed to join in the ride.

She remained silent, listening to Tommy chatter, feeling a secret rush of pleasure at Diego's easy replies, so patient and full of tenderness.

She was soon reminded of his words about this being their last day of freedom. That was evidenced by the armed guards at the gate. When she looked back at the house, she thought she saw the silhouette of a lone rifleman on one of the roofs, gazing out over the countryside. Probably keeping them in sight. But for a moment it all made her insides tremble with uncertainty.

She turned quickly, about to ask Diego, but he'd seen her turn and had followed her gaze to the lone marksman on the tiled roof.

"It's all right," he said, keeping his voice calm and normal. "One of ours."

"What?" Tommy turned his head. "What's one of ours?"

"Nothing, sweetie," Jessica said. "Just grown-up talk."

They were through the gates, cluttered now with new equipment. Though seeing the armed guards and the rifleman had given Jessica qualms, she was glad they were there. Soon she was able to shake it off. She felt safe with Diego. She always had.

The weather was perfect. She had forgotten how much she longed to get out, how much she had missed riding, how much she missed being with a man.

This man in particular.

The cottonwoods were a cool oasis after the short ride in the blazing sunlight. The gray green leaves shook in the stiff breeze, their rustling mingling pleasantly with the sound of the rushing brook nearby.

The smell of water and earth, of sun-warmed grass, quickly and unexpectedly filled Jessica with a nostalgia that almost took her breath away.

When she turned and looked at Diego, he was watching her.

She couldn't be sure if the atmosphere had brought back memories to him, but something had. She saw the flicker of recognition deep in his eyes. He was riding very close to her, their legs almost touching. For a moment, he leaned toward her and she thought he might reach out and kiss her.

She wanted it. Every inch of her body tingled with that want.

She'd never felt so alive, never felt more like a woman than when Diego looked deeply into her eyes in this, their sacred place.

"Why are you two looking so funny?" Tommy was frowning at them, his face screwed up into a puzzled grimace.

Diego threw his head back and laughed heartily as Jessica's soft tinkling laughter joined in.

"Grown-ups," Tommy declared, frowning again. "Can we eat now, Mom? Can we wade in the creek?"

"One thing at a time." Diego climbed down and helped Tommy off his pony.

Tommy immediately ran toward the creek, stopping only when Jessica called to him.

She swung her leg over the saddle. When she turned, Diego was there, his hands reaching for her. He pulled her down and turned her to face him, their bodies touching.

Jessica's breath caught in her throat, and she quickly stepped away, making a point of looking toward Tommy as if to check on him.

"Well, one thing's for sure," Diego drawled.

"What?" she asked, looking at him over her shoulder.

"After today, sharing this place with a rambunctious little boy, we may never look at it the same again."

His words were teasing. They were also a sweet reminder of what being here alone had once meant to them both. But instead of defusing the sexual tension between them, his words seemed to accelerate it.

Jessica had heard different friends speak of the changes children made in a relationship, but she hadn't known exactly what they meant until this moment.

There was an unspoken sharing between them now that was deeper, sweeter, more fulfilling than anything she'd ever imagined.

And he was right. After sharing the cottonwoods as a family, this place would never be the same for the two of them. She dared not speak what was in her heart—that she secretly prayed it would become even better.

Diego tied the horses nearby in a stand of cottonwood trees. Here near the stream, the breeze seemed lighter and a bit cooler. The fragile looking leaves whispered and rustled overhead.

Jessica found a spot near the stream for the picnic and spread a tablecloth on the ground.

Tommy ran back and forth, helping Diego carry the supplies from the horses.

This was not the exact place where Jessica and Diego had always met, the place where they'd first made love. That was further downstream and more secluded.

Both of them were better off avoiding that spot, neither acknowledging it nor looking in that direction. She wasn't sure how she'd have reacted if Diego had led them there today.

They were all laughing as they ate, sometimes at the nearby squirrels. But sometimes their laughter seemed to be for no reason at all except it was a beautiful day and they were free from the constraints of the house.

But for Jessica, the day was magical. It was the simple, quiet kind of day she might have dreamed about long ago, on those dark, lonely nights when every thought, every remembrance of Diego brought heartbreaking agony.

The only qualm she had was about their reason for being here and how they were going to tell Tommy that Diego was his father.

As it turned out, they didn't have to wait long for an opportunity.

After they'd finished eating, Jessica lay on her side, propped up on her bent elbow as she lazily watched the trembling leaves overhead and listened to the rush of the nearby stream.

Tommy scurried across the tablecloth, making himself a comfortable spot between Jessica and Diego.

"Mom, where did I come from?"

Jessica blinked and looked across into Diego's twinkling eyes.

"Well, sweetie, what do you mean? Remember once when Lady had her puppies and I explained how people have babies kind of the same way?"

"Yeah, but only one at a time."

"Usually." She laughed.

"I don't mean that."

"What did you mean, son?" Diego asked.

"Lady has Bo for a husband. Bo was the pups' dad. And our mares, they have Thunder for a husband. Grandpa said horses can have more than one wife," he added, nodding wisely at Diego.

"Ah," Diego said.

Jessica could feel her cheeks burning under Diego's amused scrutiny. She took a deep breath and shook her head, touching her cool hands to her face.

"The boy has a quick mind," Diego drawled, obviously enjoying her discomfort.

"Comes from living on a ranch, I guess."

Tommy looked from one of them to the other. He seemed a bit perplexed and completely serious.

"Come here, son," Diego said, turning serious, too.

Tommy moved over to Diego, who cradled him in one arm. The boy pushed his feet and legs out in front of him and Diego absent-mindedly brushed his hand down Tommy's jeans leg.

"I guess what you're asking about is your own

dad. Something you've wondered about for a long time, huh?"

"Yeah." Tommy looked up at Diego.

Jessica held her breath. It was such a precious moment and she didn't want to miss a second of it, yet her heart was pounding so hard it seemed to be all she could hear.

"You know I told you I lived here at the McLean ranch several years ago?"

"Before you became a Texas Ranger," Tommy said.

"That's right, and your mom and I were . . . um, good friends." Diego glanced at Jessica, rolling his eyes as if he needed help.

She smiled encouragingly at him and shrugged her shoulders.

"Good friends?" Tommy asked.

"What Diego means, sweetie," Jessica said, swallowing hard, "is that we . . . Diego and I . . . we were in love."

"In love?" Tommy asked, twisting his mouth to one side. "You mean boy and girl kind of love?"

"That's right." Diego chuckled. "Boy and girl kind of love."

"Yuck."

What now? Jessica mouthed silently, lifting her hands helplessly.

"Oh." Tommy sat up straighter, pulling slightly away from Diego and looking keenly from one of them to the other.

"You mean . . . you mean Diego's my dad? My real dad?"

Jessica's breath left her lips in a sigh of relief and her shoulders slumped forward.

"That's exactly what we mean," Diego said. "How do you feel about that?"

"I dunno," Tommy answered, shrugging. "Cool! Mom? Can I look for salamanders now?" He jumped up, his attention focused on the stream and his next adventure.

"Well." Jessica felt as if she were in a complete spin.

She glanced at Diego, who was chuckling and shaking his head. Meeting his gaze, she knew he was as relieved and as bemused by their son's reaction as she was.

"Stay where I can see you," Jessica yelled as Tommy barreled toward the creek. "And watch for snakes."

Jessica turned back to Diego.

"Is that all there is?" she asked. "Just . . . cool?"

"I doubt it." Diego turned his gaze toward Tommy. "But for now, I guess that's not a bad reaction. At least he didn't hate the idea."

"Oh, no," she said, her voice growing almost shy. "I knew he wouldn't hate it. He adores you. It's almost as if he knew all along somewhere deep down in his innocent little soul."

"You're still a dreamer," Diego said. It wasn't a condemnation. In fact, it almost sounded like a compliment.

His words gave her a quick rush of pleasure.

For a moment, it was as if they had gone back

in time to those days when nothing and no one mattered except them and their being together. The look in his eyes was so sweetly familiar.

She realized he was right. If she could still have hope in her heart that things might turn out right for them, then she was a dreamer.

TEN

Watching Tommy throw rocks into the water, Jessica and Diego had little to say. Soon the quiet, the soothing breeze, the warmth of the sun left Jessica feeling relaxed and sleepy.

She lay with her legs curled up, her arm beneath her head as she grew more and more sleepy.

"Go ahead," Diego said.

She glanced over to where he sat across from her, his back against the trunk of a tree. Even on their day of leisure, he could not be without the gun and holster at his side, and his eyes were cautious and constantly watchful as he scanned the landscape around them and the horizon beyond.

"Take a nap," he said, nodding toward Tommy. "I'll watch the boy."

She wondered at his use of the phrase "the boy." What was he thinking? And how was he feeling now that Tommy knew that Diego was his father?

At the moment Diego seemed especially far away and so closed off from her. She had no one to blame for that but herself and her father, but she had hoped their day would be different, that maybe he could put aside his anger for one day at least.

That he apparently couldn't troubled her. *He* troubled her—in more ways than one.

"What's wrong?" he asked, seeing her look. "Don't you trust me?" Even though his voice was teasing, there was a glint of that old defensiveness in his eyes when he spoke.

"I trust you," she said, her voice a little husky from sleepiness.

She trusted him more than anyone she'd ever known, but she didn't know how to make him believe that. The things that had happened to them, the events that had torn them apart, weren't necessarily their fault, not that it mattered now. The damage was done. The pain and distrust lingered between them. Sometimes the futility of it all made her want to cry.

"What's wrong, then?" Diego asked.

"Nothing." She closed her eyes as if to sleep.

"Are you having regrets?"

She opened her eyes and pushed herself up, wide awake now.

"Regrets? About telling Tommy? No, of course not. Why? Are you?"

He pursed his lips, pulling his gaze away from hers. He picked up a small twig and began making marks in the dirt.

"No," he said, glancing up only briefly. "But we do need to decide on a few things, hopefully without getting a passel of lawyers involved."

"Such as?"

"Visitations, child support—"

"There's no need for child support," she said quickly, almost defensively. "We have—"

"I'm sure there's no *need.*" His voice was dry and sarcastic. "But he's my son and I intend to pay child support, whether you need it or not. Put it in a college fund, do whatever you want to with it. But I'm paying it, one way or another."

She shook her head. "Please, don't misinterpret everything I say. It's hard enough without having to fight with you over every word I say. I thought after today we might—"

"What?" he asked coolly. "Kiss and make up? Begin all over again, here where we first started?"

She frowned at him, unable to understand the change in him.

"What is this? Why are you suddenly so angry and deliberately cruel?"

Diego clenched his jaw and stared into space, his eyes searching for Tommy.

He didn't know why he was angry. Now that it was all out in the open, he realized he wanted, needed more than just the acknowledgement that Tommy was his. He wanted those four years of his son's life back, and he wanted more from Jessica than she was willing to give.

He always had.

And that had always been the problem.

"I want this to work, Diego. I don't blame you for being angry. I wouldn't even blame you if you hated me."

"I don't hate you," he muttered. He wished he

could. God, if she only knew how wrong she was about that.

"Then what? You have what you wanted. Tommy knows you're his dad. And if you're feeling a little disappointed about his reaction—"

"I'm not disappointed." He swore softly. "I'm not as naive about children as that. I know it will take time for him to adjust and to realize exactly what all this means."

"Then can't we try to be civil to each other, for Tommy's sake, if nothing else? Even pretend a little if we have to?"

His eyes narrowed and he stared straight into her wide green eyes. "Pretend?" he asked, his voice slow and meaningful. "Exactly what did you have in mind?"

"I . . . I didn't mean that."

"Oh, guess I forgot. This is all going too fast for you. Excuse me." He got to his feet, calling over his shoulder as he walked toward the stream. "I didn't mean to overstep my bounds."

Jessica sighed and sat up. Any hope she had for a peaceful nap was gone.

He was so damned exasperating—one moment sweet and seemingly willing to do whatever it took to make things easier, and the next, stubborn and angry and downright mean.

It was getting late when they began to hear rumbles of thunder in the distance. Even though there were no storm clouds in sight, the wind had picked up, too.

In this part of Texas, summer rainstorms were few and far between. Still, one never knew.

Jessica had started gathering up their things when Diego and Tommy came to help.

"I thought I heard thunder," she said.

"Yeah, so did I," he said. "It's probably nothing. Still, we'd better head back. Can't take a chance on being stranded out here if an electrical storm is heading our way."

"Aw, do we have to?"

Jessica recognized the whine in Tommy's voice as a symptom of fatigue.

"Yes, we have to," she replied firmly. "Now get your shoes and let's get ready."

Riding back toward the house, Diego led the way. Staying close beside Tommy's pony, he pushed the horses a little harder than he had on the trip out.

Toward the west, the sky was dark. Intermittently, lightning slashed from the heavens to the ground. The storm seemed to be moving faster than either of them had anticipated.

By the time they rode into the barn, the storm was upon them.

There didn't seem to be any rain, just mostly wind and lightning and terrible crashes of thunder. In the stalls, the horses quivered, some of them moving about skittishly at each new bolt.

"We'd better stay put for a while," Diego said, glancing out at the darkening skies. "That lightning looks deadly."

Tommy was completely exhausted. When Diego

pulled him from his saddle, the boy curled up against him, wrapping his arms around his neck and resting his head against Diego's chest.

"He's wiped out," Diego said. "I'll put him on the cot back in the tack room till this is all over."

Because it was so late and close to supper time, there was no one else in the barn. "While you do that, I'll take care of the horses," Jessica said.

Lightning periodically illuminated the barn's shadowy interior, and when it faded away, the barn seemed even darker than before.

She heard Diego coming up behind her and turned to meet him.

"Pretty bad storm," Diego said, picking up a comb to help her with the horses.

"I hope Dad isn't worried. Maybe I should try and make it to the house to let him know we're all right."

"No way." Diego shook his head. "This storm is so fierce I'm not sure we're even safe here inside the barn."

"We had lightning rods installed a few years back." She glanced up through the rafters high above them.

"That's good." He seemed quieter, less angry than he had been at the creek.

"Jessica," he began, when they'd finished caring for the horses, "I'm sorry if I seemed on edge back there. It has nothing to do with you."

"I understand," she said. That was a lie, of course. She didn't understand, but she didn't want to start another fight.

She was standing with her back against an empty stall, hugging her arms across her breasts. Diego was only a few feet away.

He pushed his fingers through his hair, his gaze moving from one place in the barn to the other. "I'm glad we had the chance to take Tommy out today."

"Yes, so am I."

"Once they serve the papers on Colby, our security measures will go up. It could get scary, although the worst I'm hoping for is just plain boredom. Today was probably your last chance at freedom for a while."

"I know." She looked down, scuffing the toe of her boot in the dirt. "You, too, though," she added, her voice soft.

"I know, but it's my job. I'm used to long, boring stakeouts."

"Sure." She clamped her lips tightly together.

"Hell," he muttered. Why was talking to her so difficult? It didn't used to be. "You know, this is all new to me. I've never been in the position of guarding someone I knew . . . or cared about." He lifted his hands in a gesture of frustration. "It takes on a new perspective. Makes me a little edgy."

"Tommy, you mean," she said, her voice breathless.

His head came up and he looked straight into her wide, questioning eyes.

"I think you know exactly what I mean, Jess."

Jessica's lips trembled. Against her will, tears

pooled in her eyes. She'd been fighting back tears from the first moment he came back. Finally, she found herself powerless to stop them from spilling down her cheeks.

"Oh, heck, I don't know why I'm crying. It seems like all I've done lately. You must think I've lost my mind."

He frowned, hearing the pain in her voice. She *had* seemed on the verge of tears several times in the past few days, not that he always understood why. One thing he did know, this was no game she was playing. Her tears and her pain were genuine.

He didn't have to think about his next move. It just seemed to happen.

"Jess," Diego said, his voice rough with emotion.

He stepped toward her, one hand reaching to touch her hair and the side of her face. With his thumb, he wiped away her tears then pulled her toward him.

"Of course I don't think you've lost your mind." His voice was soothing and sweet. He touched her hair, sinking his fingers into the silky strands and pulling her head to his chest. "This has been hard for all of us."

She felt so small in his arms, so delicate. So right. Her hair smelled of sun and wind, but her appeal today was more than that. There was that familiar spark between them, one that tantalized with every touch, every look. Diego's body tightened. The old desire resurfaced, quick and urgent.

Jessica surprised even herself, snuggling against

him with no hesitation, letting him soothe her and stroke her hair as if she were a child.

"If I said something earlier to upset you—"

"No." She moved her head back and forth against his shirt. "It's just . . . when you're nice to me, I . . . I just can't take it."

"My being nice upsets you?" he asked, smiling. He let his hands move down her back to the delicate curve of her spine. The memory of last night and the way she had kissed him, then retreated, came back in a rush. He didn't want to take a chance on pushing her away again, but he was quickly moving past the point where he could still pull away from her.

She pulled back a little, tilting her head to look up into his face. Her face was set and the traces of tears in her eyes turned them the color of glittering emeralds.

"Because I know . . ." She made a quiet hiccuping sound, like a little girl. "I know I don't deserve your kindness," she whispered, her lips trembling as if she might begin to cry again.

"Jessie." He couldn't help what happened next any more than he could have stopped himself from breathing.

His mouth covered hers, hot and hungry. He heard and felt her small gasp as she pushed herself against him, her hands embracing his face before moving up into his hair.

The raging storm outside faded into the background and there was nothing, no one except the two of them and the glory of being together.

He claimed her mouth again and again and she answered him as if she couldn't get enough. She strained against him until finally he pushed her back against the wooden boards of the stall, trapping her there, enjoying the sensuous feel of every inch of her body against his. He ground his hips into hers to let her know exactly how much he needed her.

"God, Jessie," he growled, pulling away from her hot, desperate lips. "I want you so damned much."

She whispered his name, tugging at his shirt until she could move her hands up beneath the material. His skin was on fire and her fingers felt cool, like the quick fleeting dance of a butterfly.

She was driving him crazy. His whispered words were those of wild sexual desire, until he hardly knew what he was saying. He was only aware of what he was feeling and what he wanted, and those desires were so intense he couldn't hear or feel anything else.

His hands moved down to her hips, pulling her hard against him until she was gasping for breath.

Their movements were those of lovers. Only the layers of clothing that separated their bodies kept them from doing what they really wanted.

For a moment Diego actually considered ripping away her shirt, stripping her and taking what he wanted.

It wasn't even something he had to say out loud. She knew instinctively what he was thinking.

"Yes," she whispered, her lips hot against his ear. "Oh, Diego, it's been so long . . . so—"

The thunder drowned out her words, but somewhere in the back of her mind, she heard another, more familiar sound.

One she couldn't ignore.

"Mommy."

Slowly, reluctantly, like a woman drugged, she pulled herself away from Diego's arms, away from his warm, tempting mouth.

"It's Tommy," she whispered, her voice shaky. She was leaning against him, her arms curved up beneath his and wrapped around him. "I . . . we have to go."

He moaned and pulled her back for one last kiss. His eyes were dark like evening storm clouds, and the look on his face told her he could hardly bear to let her go.

"I have to." She reached out to touch his lips.

"I know. Go. He'll be afraid."

He watched her go, taking long deep breaths of air, trying to slow the pounding of his heart and cool his raging blood.

He walked back and forth, glancing from time to time down the darkened corridor toward the shaft of light coming from the tack room.

How in hell had this happened after he had promised himself it wouldn't?

He'd known when she asked for time last night that he needed to distance himself from her. He needed some time, too. It was too easy to fall back into this soft, sensual web. He couldn't believe he had let himself do it again.

Even when he was working around the ranch,

he'd find himself thinking of her. Inevitably there would come that quick sudden urge to find her and the never forgotten memories of making love to her.

Anything could remind him of her. Here on the McLean ranch, where it had all started, *everything* reminded him of her. Those memories could send him spiraling back to the sensual contrasts of their lovemaking, her pale softness next to his harder, darker body.

He hadn't intended this to happen, not again. Now that it had, it wouldn't be easy to forget or to ignore—for either of them.

GET STARTED TODAY –
NO RISK AND NO OBLIGATION

To get your introductory gift of 4 Free Bouquet Romances fill out and mail the enclosed Free Book Certificate today. We'll ship your free selections as soon as we receive this information. Remember that you are under no obligation. This is a risk free offer from the publishers of
Zebra Bouquet Romances.

FREE BOOK CERTIFICATE

Yes! I would like to take you up on your offer. Please send me 4 Free Bouquet Romance Novels as my introductory gift. I understand that unless I tell you otherwise, I will then receive the 4 newest Bouquet novels to preview each month Free for 10 days. If I decide to keep them I'll pay the preferred home subscriber's price of just $3.20 each (a total of only $12.80) plus $1.50 for shipping and handling. That's a 20% savings off the publisher's price. I understand that I may return any shipment for full credit no questions asked and I may cancel this subscription at any time with no obligation. Regardless of what I decide to do, the 4 Free introductory novels are mine to keep as Bouquet's gift.

Name _____

Address _____ Apt. _____

City _____ State _____ Zip _____

Telephone ( ) _____

Signature _____ BN010R
(If under 18, parent or guardian must sign.)

For your convenience you may charge your shipments automatically to a Visa or MasterCard so you'll never have to worry about late payments and missing shipments. If you return any shipment we'll credit your account.

Yes, charge my credit card for my "Bouquet Romance" shipments until I tell you otherwise.
☐ Visa ☐ MasterCard

Account Number _____

Expiration Date _____

Signature _____

Orders subject to acceptance by Zebra Home Subscription Service. Terms and Prices subject to change.
Offer valid in U.S. only.

BOUQUET ROMANCE
120 Brighton Road
P.O. BOX 5214
Clifton, New Jersey 07015-5214

AFFIX
STAMP
HERE

ELEVEN

As Diego waited for Jessica, he realized he was becoming completely obsessed with her—making excuses to see her, to touch her, vowing one minute not to be near her and the next unable to keep his hands off her.

She could be so cool sometimes, but underneath it all, he knew the real Jessica, the one full of passion and love and contradictions.

She could retreat within herself if she felt threatened or hurt, and maybe subconsciously his masculine ego made him want to break through that facade, to get to the real Jessica. He wanted to be the only man who could.

He wanted to see those clear green eyes grow shadowy and languid, wanted to see her mouth become soft and sensual.

All for him.

Hell, he might as well admit it. Having her was becoming an obsession, and that could be disastrous for both of them—and for Tommy.

He could hear Jessica and Tommy in the tack

room, and he used that time to try and cool himself off.

It wasn't easy.

He wanted her. Surprisingly, it was more than physical wanting, more than pure lust this time. He wanted her to give herself to him, mind, body, and soul. He also wanted . . . needed . . . her to trust him, to look into his eyes with an open, vulnerable look that said she was willing to give more than she knew she should.

This time, here alone with her, he'd been so close. He'd felt her resolve weakening. He'd seen it in her eyes.

He couldn't help envisioning them together. All the memories came pouring over him of her beneath him, her beautiful eyes never leaving his face, her soft little cries of passion, and the way she could give herself so completely and still hold something of herself back.

Damn it, he wanted all of her this time, with nothing held back.

But he had to wonder about what had just happened between them. She had been just as aroused as he was. That much he was sure of.

But now what? Was it the same old story, that he was good enough to sleep with? When it was all over, would she turn her back on him again, remember who he was and who she was and decide it could never work?

As much as he wanted her, he'd be a fool to let that happen again.

Jessica stepped into the corridor, carrying Tommy in her arms.

Diego took a deep breath, trying to banish the memories and the fantasies. As he watched her walk toward him, he brushed his arm across his forehead, as if trying to clear some imaginary veil from his eyes.

Jessica stopped in front of him and looked up into his face. She thought that hungry look still smoldered deep down in his eyes. As always, that subtle, mysterious hint of danger was there, had been even before he became a Ranger.

It was something she didn't understand about him, and she wasn't sure she ever would. Years ago it had made him alluring and appealing. Even now, she felt that same allure—especially after his kiss.

He could have no doubt now about how much she wanted him. If he had wondered before about her reluctance, he certainly shouldn't be wondering now.

Tommy, his head resting against Jessica's chest, turned and looked sleepily at Diego. Then he reached out his arms to him.

With a murmur of tenderness that surprised Jessica, Diego accepted Tommy readily. It was as if cuddling a small boy was the most natural thing in the world to him.

Just for a moment before she released Tommy, the three of them stood linked together, one of Tommy's arms around Jessica, the other around Diego.

Diego pulled the boy into his arms, brushing his lips across Tommy's dark tousled hair and looking for a moment into Jessica's awe-filled eyes.

He couldn't help wondering what she expected from him now. What could he give without revealing his entire soul?

"I think the storm has passed," she said.

"Yeah, we should get back to the house, get this boy in bed." He jostled Tommy affectionately.

Jessica nodded and moved toward the door. Diego followed, carrying Tommy. If she resented having to share her son after all this time of having him to herself, there was no hint of it in her expression. In fact, sometimes Diego thought he saw a hint of genuine pleasure on her face when he and Tommy were especially close.

"You tired, cowboy?" Diego asked the boy.

"Hungry," Tommy muttered.

"Yeah? I'll bet Rosie will have something good waiting for you."

"Will you read me a story before I go to bed?" Tommy asked.

"Well, I have a bit of work to do. Tell you what, why don't you eat supper, then take your bath. By the time you're finished, I should be back. I'll read you a story then. How's that?"

Tommy sighed with pure contentment and nodded, nuzzling his face against Diego's neck.

Jessica stood at the door, holding it open and waiting for them. Diego brushed against her as he passed, and when she reached out to touch

Tommy's hair, he felt the touch of her fingers across his shoulder and down his arm.

Inside the house, everyone was relieved to see them back safe and sound.

Diego put Tommy down and Rosie took the boy's hand.

"We were so worried about you," she said. She handed a small piece of paper to Diego. "Your captain called and left this message."

Rosie led Tommy toward the kitchen, then glanced back over her shoulder at Jessica and Diego, who remained in the hallway, watching Tommy. Rosie's gaze was questioning and there was a little smile on her face as if she knew something no one else knew, but she said nothing.

Alone in the hallway, a strained awkwardness grew between Jessica and Diego.

Jessica wanted to touch him again, wanted him to pull her into his arms with that hungry shudder of passion. She wanted to feel the irresistible heat rising between them, wanted to give herself up to it completely. It had been so long since she'd felt such delicious ecstasy, and there had been times the past few years when she wondered if she'd ever feel it again.

She waited, looking for the slightest hint in his eyes that it was what he wanted, too.

"The captain says Colby is in custody and everything's a go," Diego said. "I need to check all the equipment, make sure the electrical storm didn't short anything out."

"What about Tommy?"

"I'll be back in time to read him a story. I'll make time. But right now I have to do this—it's important."

"I know."

How could he be so cool, she wondered, so businesslike after what had happened between them in the barn? Now that he knew how much she wanted him in return, why did she have this feeling he was backing off?

The thought that he'd changed his mind sent a pang of disappointment tearing through Jessica's heart.

"Looks like this is it, Jessie." He shook the piece of paper absentmindedly. "From here on in, we all have to be on guard every minute. If they hold Colby without bond the way we're hoping, we've got no problem. But if not . . ." He shrugged his broad shoulders and rubbed his hand down his jaw.

"I trust you to take care of us," she said, still feeling that closeness, that bond between them, and wanting to hear him acknowledge he felt it, too.

"I'm afraid it will take more than trust more than trust." His face grew a bit gentler. "I'm going to need you to do everything I say, Jess. I know you're used to having your freedom and independence, used to doing things your own way here. But until this is settled, you have to run everything past me and do exactly as I say."

"I have no problem with that." She surprised herself by saying it, but at the moment, she trusted him completely to do what was right for all of them.

He looked down at her for a moment, there in the shadows of the hallway.

"Well." He turned away. "I'd better get to work."

"But what about supper? Don't you have time to sit down and—"

"I'll grab something on the way out. You go ahead."

He was gone, leaving her alone and feeling as if she'd been caught in an unexpected whirlwind.

She watched him go, unable to understand what had just happened between them. She was still standing there when Rosie returned.

"Did Diego leave?"

"Yes." Jessica waved her hand toward the door. "He . . . he said he had some work to do. Something about possible damage from the electrical storm."

"It was a fierce one, wasn't it? I told your daddy you're back. He's already had his supper, but he's in the study if you'd like to go in and say good night."

"Yes, I will," Jessica said. But her mind wasn't on her father. She walked to a nearby table and plucked at the fresh flowers arranged in a large earthenware jug.

"He was worried, thinking you might be stranded out in the open."

Jessica made a quiet sound and shrugged her shoulders.

"Your picnic is all little Tommy can talk about." Rosie looked closer at Jessica. "He's more excited than I've ever seen him."

"Oh, he loved every minute of it." Jessica pulled a small rose from the arrangement of flowers and plucked distractedly at its petals.

"And you?"

Jessica looked up, as if she hadn't really heard Rosie's question.

"Me?" she asked. "Yes, I enjoyed it, too. It was beautiful by the creek. The weather was wonderful and it was great seeing Tommy enjoy himself that way."

"Then why do you have that sad look on your face?"

Jessica sighed and shook her head, tossing the rose back onto the table.

"We told Tommy today that Diego is his dad."

"Oh, Jessica, honey." Rosie clasped her hands together and lifted them to her chin. "That's wonderful. How did he take it? I'm sure that explains his excitement."

"Actually"—there was a bemused look on Jessica's face as she remembered Tommy's reaction—"he didn't have a lot to say. 'Cool' about covers it, I think." She smiled wryly at Rosie. "But I do think he's happy about it."

She remembered how Tommy had reached for Diego so sweetly in the barn. Even Diego's demeanor had seemed to change today. Perhaps it was just the open acknowledgement that Tommy was his. Obviously, Tommy had accepted Diego right away. He was a sweet, open little boy, and Jessica didn't think he would have any problem welcoming Diego into his life.

"Yes, Tommy is definitely excited, but I'm sure he's a little confused, too. He's too young to understand all this."

"It will take time," Rosie agreed, nodding wisely. "And what about you and Diego? Was this the new beginning we talked about?"

"I . . . I thought it might be." Jessica frowned as she looked into Rosie's dark eyes. "But, now that we're back in this house, he seems so different, so cool and businesslike, as if nothing at all happened between us."

Rosie gave a quiet murmur of sympathy.

"I just don't know anymore, Rosie. I don't know what he wants or what he expects. One minute he's warm and sweet and protective and the next . . ." She waved her hands in the air.

"He's been hurt." Rosie deliberately kept her voice sympathetic. "It will take time for him."

"I've been hurt, too," Jessica said, more defensively than she intended. Her lips trembled slightly and she clamped them together in a determined line. "My whole life changed when Tommy was born, and it's been no picnic raising him alone. Never mind." She sighed. "I don't want to get into that. It wasn't Diego's fault, and it wasn't mine. I need to be alone for a while, Rosie. Will you see that Tommy has a bath when he's finished eating? Diego promised to be back in time to read him a bedtime story."

"Sure, I'll be happy to. You go ahead, spend a little time by yourself."

Jessica stopped by the study just long enough to say hello to her father and let him know they were all right.

She didn't want to talk to him right now. She didn't want to talk to anyone.

She hurried outside, looking around, wondering where Diego was. It wasn't that she wanted to see him. In fact, she didn't know what she would say if she did.

She ended up in the barn, where it was still quiet. For a moment she stood in the same spot where they'd kissed. Closing her eyes, she gave in to all the emotions she'd been feeling. She let herself relive it all, experience the joy and the passion his kiss and his touch had brought.

When she opened her eyes, it was growing dark outside and she felt a little shiver move over her skin. It was too cool to linger there in the barn doing nothing.

She found a pitchfork and began forking straw into one of the empty stalls. There was no need for her to do any of this. There were enough hired hands on the ranch to keep the barn spotless and in good working order.

Normally if she were restless, she might ride out alone, let the wind and night air whisk all the cobwebs from her brain, let herself feel nothing except the horse beneath her and the endless miles of emptiness around her. But, as Diego had warned earlier, things had changed. She might not be safe, and he would have a fit if she went against his wishes.

Still, she had to do something physical to take away some of the tension she felt. She attacked the straw with renewed purpose.

When she finally went back to the house, it was late and she was exhausted, her goal accomplished. She would take a quick shower and check on Tommy before he went to sleep.

After her shower, she pulled on a soft cotton knit dress and tied her damp hair back. Then she knocked on the door separating her room from Diego's. At first she had found it awkward having to go through his room to get to Tommy's, but now she welcomed it, knowing it would give her an excuse to see him and be near him.

There was no answer. She knocked again.

Finally, still hearing nothing, she opened the door and peeped into his room. It was dark and empty, and she could see no sign he had even been here.

A small tingle of alarm raced down her spine. Then, seeing the light spilling across the floor from Tommy's room, she told herself Diego was probably with Tommy already, reading him that bedtime story.

She hurried across the room, slowing at Tommy's door before stepping inside.

One of the girls sat beside the bed, a book in her hands. She looked up when Jessica came in and smiled, then motioned her forward.

Tommy's dark hair shone brightly in the light of

the lamp. Stepping closer, Jessica saw his eyes were closed and his chest rose gently in sleep.

"He's just gone to sleep," the girl said.

"He was exhausted."

"You need me to stay longer?"

"No, Sheila. I'll stay with him until Diego gets here." She hoped her voice sounded nonchalant when she continued. "Was Diego here earlier? He was going to read to Tommy."

"No, I haven't seen him. After supper, Tommy played a little, then took his bath. Rosie went to talk to the cook about tomorrow's menus. There's been no one else here except me."

"I see. Well, go ahead, Sheila, and thank you for staying late."

"You're welcome." The girl rose and left the room.

Jessica frowned.

Where was Diego? Something important must have happened for him to go back on his word to his son, even if it involved a small thing like reading a book.

Several minutes later, she heard a door open. Getting up and going to the doorway, she saw Diego walk into his room. He saw her immediately and acknowledged her presence with a curt nod. His thumbs moved up beneath the shoulder holster; he slid it off and hung it on a nearby chair, then he massaged his neck and shoulders before coming to stand within a few feet of Jessica.

"Is the boy asleep?"

His words infuriated her. "Yes, the *boy*, as you

call him, is asleep. He probably cried himself to sleep when you failed to show up and read to him as you promised."

Diego frowned at her, then made a humorous noise in his throat before pushing his way past her. He leaned over Tommy, pulling the covers up a little bit, then turning out the lamp beside the bed. A night-light came on, throwing a warm, yellow glow across the floor.

"How could you do this?" she asked. "The first night he realizes he has a father, you abandon him."

He turned sharply to her. This time there was no hint of humor in his features or his dark eyes.

He took her by the arm, leading her from the room and pulling the door partly closed behind them.

"What in hell is this all about? You're furious because I didn't get back in time to read a bedtime story?"

"Yes, I'm furious. You promised. And in this family, we keep our promises." She stopped almost before she got the words out, knowing how pious and self-righteous they must sound to him.

But not before Diego threw back his head and gave a short bark of laughter.

"And what promises would that be?" he drawled. "To lie and cheat? To look down their noses on the rest of the world whenever possible?"

"That is not fair," she said, fuming.

"Baby, whoever said life was fair didn't have an idea in hell what they were talking about."

"How could you treat him this way? How could you disappoint him?"

"For God's sake, Jessica, it's just a bedtime story. The boy's going to experience a few disappointments in his life. The storm knocked out a major connection between the cameras and the monitors here in the house. We had to install an override switch so it won't happen again. I'll explain everything to Tommy tomorrow."

"Oh, I'm sure that will do it. Just give him one of your cool, reasonable Texas Ranger explanations."

"It's better than catering to his every whim and turning him into a spoiled, selfish rich kid."

"Like his mother, you mean."

"Your words." He turned away from her. "Not mine."

"I thought I knew you," she said, her voice breaking with emotion. "But I'm not sure I ever knew you at all."

"God, what do you want from me, Jessica?" He faced her, the fury in his eyes nailing her to the spot. "You want me to be Tommy's Dad now? Be the man, the teacher he never had? I'm playing catch-up here, you know. And what about you, Jess? Do you want me to be your friend, your protector? Or do you want more?"

He reached out, grabbing her arms and pulling her toward him until she was trembling.

"You're still playing at this, Jess, experimenting with the poor boy from the wrong side of town."

"How can you say that to me?"

"How can I not?"

She stared into his eyes, unable to believe the fury that raced through both of them. It was as if a flame arced from one of them to the other, grounding them both to the floor.

"Let go of me."

He continued to hold her until she jerked at his hands, fury sparking in her eyes.

"I mean it, Diego. Let me go."

He took a deep breath, his laughter forced and harsh, his eyes glinting. Then he released her, throwing his arms out and remaining that way, arrogant and cold as she pushed her way past him.

When she closed the door to her room, she was shaking so badly her legs would barely hold her.

Then she began to cry, her sobs coming hard and uncontrollably as she slid down the door onto the floor. She'd needed to cry since they left the barn today, and she'd pushed it away. Now there was no stopping the fury and anguish of her tears.

For a while today she had felt happy, felt a glimmer of hope for the future, for the first time in a long time. She had no idea what Diego thought of her or what he thought she'd been doing all these years since he left.

But she remembered the loneliness before Tommy was born, the long desperate, dark nights when she realized she had lost the one man she had ever loved.

Having a child alone was not something she'd ever wish on any woman. That was something meant to be shared with the man you loved.

There had been times afterward when she tried to move on with her life—a few dates, some dances at the club, a few kisses from men she'd grown up with or from men who knew who she was and how much wealth she would one day acquire.

None of them had ever moved her, and none had ever come remotely close to making her feel a tenth of what Diego made her feel.

That much hadn't changed, it seemed. Sometimes she wondered if it ever would.

TWELVE

Diego stood for a moment, stunned, as he stared at the closed door to Jessica's bedroom.

"Damn it." He pushed both hands through his hair, pressing against the side of his head and down the back of his neck.

Finally he walked to the door, placing one hand against the wood panel and trying to turn the knob with the other.

He wasn't surprised to find it locked.

"Jess? Jessica. Open the door."

"Go away," she said, her voice muffled and heavy.

"Jessica." He cursed under his breath. "Are you crying?"

"No," she shouted. Her voice was choked with tears and it was obvious she was lying. "Just go away. Leave me alone."

He turned around once, like a man lost. He felt like kicking himself. He hadn't meant to make her cry. But now what he really wanted to do was kick down the damned door and make her listen to him for once.

Instead he cursed furiously through clenched teeth. He wasn't sure who he was angrier with, her or himself. They couldn't seem to have a normal conversation any more.

But he was in the wrong and he knew it. He should have come back in time to read to Tommy, the way he'd promised. Of course the boy was disappointed. He couldn't blame him. But Jessica's anger was prompted by more than his failure to read a book, and he had lashed out at her from pure frustration.

After all the time he'd spent wanting her, today he'd had the chance. He knew that without a doubt. He'd seen it in her eyes, heard it in her voice, felt it when she kissed him.

And he had been stupid enough to turn away from that.

Why?

He groaned and sank down on the side of the bed, his head in his hands.

Everything about this place reminded him of Jessica, his princess of that magical summer, the girl who had loved him so completely, so trustingly.

Because of his mistakes, that sweet, innocent girl no longer existed.

She had always looked so cool, even on the hottest summer days, with her pale blond hair tied back or swept up underneath a hat.

And yet when they first made love, there had been the most amazing transformation. He'd loved tangling his fingers in her hair, setting it loose to tumble about her shoulders, wild and free. Her mouth, pale and sweet, lost its innocence and became swollen from his kisses.

God, but she had driven him wild.

That summer he couldn't imagine anything could ever come between them, couldn't imagine there'd come a day when they couldn't reach out to one another, touch one another, talk about anything, laugh about nothing.

Since his return, he thought he'd seen the promise of those times again. But then they would disappear like smoke on a cold, windy day.

Diego stood up and, with a heavy sigh, walked to Tommy's bedroom. He went in and sat on a chair beside the bed.

"I'm sorry I let you down, son," he whispered. "I should have found a way—at least sent word I couldn't make it. I guess I have a lot to learn about being a dad."

Tommy stirred and turned over. Still sleeping, he reached out one chubby hand across the bed, almost as if he'd heard and understood Diego's words.

"I'll never let anyone hurt you, cowboy," Diego said. "I swear. I will keep you safe no matter what it takes."

Jessica sat on the floor for a long while, her back against the door. She cried until she was spent, until every muscle in her body felt limp and useless.

When she finally pulled herself up, she felt light-headed and weak, but at least she wasn't sad.

No, damn it, she was mad.

Diego had been a jerk. She was certain he had deliberately waited until it was too late to read the book just to spite her.

Of course, she had picked a fight for practically no good reason. Reading a bedtime story wasn't a big deal. Tommy might have been disappointed, but he'd gone to sleep easily enough. If he'd been overly troubled, he'd have stayed awake for hours, if necessary, waiting for his dad.

But he'd been asleep when she came, obviously not upset, obviously not crying himself to sleep.

"Well, to hell with it." She wiped her eyes.

She took another shower, deliberately leaving the water cool and letting it wash over her hot, swollen face for several minutes.

When she dragged herself to bed, she couldn't sleep. She was still too pent up, too angry, and she couldn't stop listening for any sound from the room next door. One minute she hoped Diego would knock on her door and ask for her forgiveness. The next, she'd curse him beneath her breath, telling herself she didn't care if he ever spoke to her again.

But she knew that wasn't true.

Though it was almost dawn, she lay awake, her mind reeling, her body tense and anxious.

What *did* she want from him? It was the question he had asked last night.

"I want you, damn it," she muttered into the

darkness. "How could I have made it any clearer than I did in the barn? Do I have to say it out loud? Be the first to admit it?" She sighed and pushed herself up in bed, staring toward the closed door. The house was quiet now; only the muffled sound of crickets and night birds penetrated the windows and thick walls.

"You leave a woman with no pride at all, Diego Serrat," she said, her voice soft and wistful. "What am I supposed to do? Tell you how I feel and then stand there while you laugh in my face?"

Diego was a man consumed by pride. No man could guard his feelings better than Diego, and yet he didn't seem to understand that she had pride, too.

"Enough." She swung her legs over the edge of the bed.

She needed to be alone, to think and just feel her emotions and her anger. She felt on display, as if someone were always looking at her, trying to decide what she was thinking and what she would do. She had to get out of here, out of this house and away from everyone's watchful eyes.

She dressed hurriedly, glancing out the windows, hoping she would be able to get out of the house before anyone was awake, especially Diego. He'd said yesterday was their last chance to go outside the protective barriers and gates. He'd be furious if he knew what she intended to do.

But she didn't care. This was something she had to do for herself. At this point, a little time alone was like a drug she had to have. And no one, not even the powerful Diego Serrat, was going to stop her from going.

She grabbed a backpack and quickly scribbled a note for Rosie, asking her to look after Tommy for the day.

Then she headed to the kitchen, hurrying, knowing the cook was probably already awake and would be in the kitchen any moment. She wasn't trying to hide anything; she was simply tired of everyone knowing her problems, looking at her curiously, or asking where she was going.

She didn't take much food, knowing she'd be back by midafternoon. Stuffing everything into her pack, she hurried out the door. She didn't know what she would tell Hank at the front gate, but she would think of something.

She hurried to the barn and saddled her horse, then rode out to the main gate.

As it turned out, she didn't have to worry about Hank. He wasn't there. But one of the Rangers started to pick up the phone to call Diego.

Jessica frowned at him. "Don't do that. He was up with Tommy all night," she lied. "Let him rest."

"He said no one was to pass through these gates without his OK," the young Ranger said. "We're supposed to go into full protective security today."

"I know that." Jessica hoped she sounded her haughty best. "I told Diego I'd be back before that happens. And I will. He knows I'm leaving." She felt a twinge of guilt at the lie and the trouble she knew this young man would be in when Diego found out.

The Ranger frowned at Jessica and she could see the uncertainty in his eyes.

"Well, go ahead. If you want to call and wake him up, it's your responsibility, not mine."

"You sure you'll be back in a couple of hours?"

"Positive," Jessica said, a smile beginning to break across her beautiful face.

He just waved his hand at her as if he were shooing a fly.

Jessica laughed and nudged the heels of her boots into the horse's side. Within seconds, they were through the gate and out into the open. For a few moments, Jessica gave the horse his head, letting him run and loosen the tension in his strong, powerful muscles.

The sun was just coming up over the eastern mountains. The wind whipped at her hair and stung her face. It howled past her ears like a banshee, and she loved it. She hadn't felt this free in ages. She threw her head back and laughed out loud, letting the horse run, feeling his muscles ripple beneath her legs.

In a few minutes, when she pulled gently at the reins, he still wanted to run, but she didn't want to wind him. She slowed him to a trot and patted him on the neck.

"Good old Cowpoke. That's a good boy. Now that you have that out of your system, we're just going to take it easy the rest of the day. That OK with you?"

The horse whinnied as if he actually understood, and Jessica laughed again. She was well out of sight of the house now. As she relaxed in the saddle, she gazed out over the dry, almost barren land. A few bluebells still danced in the wind and clumps of tall desert grass swayed back and forth slowly. The wind was already hot, coming out of the south. When she climbed a long, sloping hill to a dry plateau, she could see for miles out over the desert. She could see most of the McLean ranch, its outbuildings clustered neatly near the house, its fenced boundaries stretching for miles on all four sides.

Here there were cedar breaks, thickets of junipers that smelled spicy and sensual and where, on hot sweltering days, a few animals might gather to sleep until the cooler winds of night came.

Jessica loved it out here. She always had. She didn't think she could tolerate the lush green forests of the east. But, of course, this was where she'd grown up. It was what she knew and loved. Some people might find it too hot, too barren and dry. But she lived here year-round and could see the changing seasons in the delicate bloom of desert flowers and cactus. They didn't get much rain, but when they did, the land would be transformed, with varieties of green grass sprouting up to blow in the wind with the bluebells and Indian paintbrush.

She spent most of the day like that, just wandering, letting her eyes take in the unique beauty of the plains, watching for antelope and deer. Once,

finding large cougar tracks, she led the horse off
in another direction. No need to borrow trouble.

She found a small stream near noon and tied
her horse nearby, while she splashed water on her
neck and face. She let the horse rest and graze
while she sat beneath a small mesquite tree to eat
her lunch. It didn't offer much shade, but it was
better than nothing.

As she sat staring out over the countryside, her
thoughts turned to Diego and their argument last
night. It seemed so long ago. Today, riding and
feeling the wind in her hair, she had managed to
avoid thinking about him. But now, in the peace
and quiet, he seemed to be all she could think
about.

Her horse grazed contentedly nearby. "Time to
go back, Cowpoke," she said. The horse turned
his head toward her for a moment, then went back
to eating.

"I can't run away from him, no matter how far
I ride, no matter where I go. The only way I'm
ever going to solve this is to face it head-on," she
told the horse. "I'm going to tell Diego how I feel.
At least then it will be out in the open and he
can do whatever he wants to about it. At least I'll
know."

She felt as if a great burden had been lifted
from her.

She gathered up her things and untied the
horse. She'd stayed longer than she intended and
in wandering had traveled further to the south
than she meant to.

Later, when she rode back onto McLean property, she knew the path she was on would take her by the stream where they had picnicked yesterday. But before that, if she didn't change her course, it would take her right by the cottonwood stand where she and Diego used to meet.

She took a deep breath. If she intended to meet her past and her emotions head-on, what better place to begin than the shelter of the cottonwoods?

A slight breeze rustled the leaves above them, causing Cowpoke to buck a little.

"Hey, what's wrong with you?" Cowpoke had always been high strung, but despite that he was one of Jessica's favorites. When he saw her come into the paddock, he always poked his nose over the fence, pleading with big brown eyes for her to choose him.

Somehow he reminded her of herself when she was a little girl. How many times had she stood watching her dad get ready to leave the house? She imagined she'd had the same look on her face as Cowpoke—the reason, perhaps, she was never able to resist him.

She laughed softly at her whimsical thoughts.

She pulled the reins, turning the horse beneath the trees and underneath a low-hanging limb. Just as she swung her leg over the saddle to dismount, a rattle made her blood run cold.

Cowpoke heard it, too, and bucked again.

"Whoa. Easy there, Pokey." Her eyes scanned the ground around them.

A katydid flew from the tree and she smiled and breathed a sigh of relief. But when Cowpoke heard it and saw it fly past, he bucked violently.

Jessica had one leg in the stirrup and was already off balance. Cowpoke was clearly past the point where he could be calmed. The only thing she could do was push herself away from him and try to jump clear. She did, but one foot landed against a rock, turning her ankle and throwing her to the ground. Cowpoke took off across the stream, bucking and twisting like an animal possessed.

"Pokey! Wait! Whoa!" She watched helplessly as he crashed through the bushes and disappeared beyond another stand of trees.

She pushed herself up off the ground and tested her ankle, trying to put her weight onto it. Pain shot up her leg to the side of her knee. Groaning, she sank down to the ground.

She couldn't believe it—thrown from her horse and left in the middle of nowhere with no food, no water, and a twisted ankle to boot.

"Worse than a city slicker," she muttered, stretching her injured leg out in front of her.

"He'll be back." She tried to reassure herself. "As soon as he runs himself into a lather, he'll come back for me." But she didn't believe it.

In the meantime, she glanced around her, looking for snakes, something the katydid had put into her own mind as well as Cowpoke's. She pulled a dead tree limb toward her, breaking it off and using it as a crutch as she pushed herself to her feet. Then she used the end of it to clear the ground beneath one of the trees.

She reached into her shirt pocket where she usually kept matches. Feeling the flat waterproof box she always carried made her feel a little better. At least she could build a fire if she had to stay here after dark.

She hobbled around, gathering firewood just in case. Then, with a sigh, she settled herself on the ground, leaning back against the tree. She was thankful she wasn't stranded in the desert. At least here she had some shelter from the sun and a light breeze to keep the heat at bay.

"Nothing I can do now except sit and wait." Still, she looked off into the distance in the direction the horse had run. She whistled and waited, listening, but there was no answering sound and no sign of Cowpoke.

"Damn," she muttered.

THIRTEEN

When Diego leaned Jessica was gone, he was angry, then frustrated. They should have talked this through last night, but both of them were still too wary and too distrustful. They were like moths dancing before a flame, reaching out, wanting to touch, to connect, but then fluttering away.

Diego blamed himself for that. If he wanted things resolved between himself and Jessica, he had to let go of the past and let himself trust again.

"You want us to go look for her?" Hank asked. He was the one who told Diego that Jessica had ridden out at sunup.

"No, let her be. Hopefully a few more hours without the security system in place won't make a difference. Rosie says she's supposed to be back by noon."

But when noon came and went and there was no sign of Jessica, Diego became restless and irritable. He tried to keep busy, tried to distract himself from thinking about her, but that wasn't easy.

By mid afternoon, Diego had become quiet. Too

quiet, some of his men noted. When Diego Serrat was quiet, he could be dangerous. He was stony faced, and often he'd look up from whatever he was doing and gaze toward the gates, as if expecting to see someone riding in.

"I swear," Rosie said, watching out of the windows, "that man is like a smoldering volcano about to blow—scary and way too quiet."

It was past five o'clock when Diego walked out to the gate, where a small watchtower had been constructed in the last week. It was now manned and ready. He could see one of his men up there now.

Diego jogged up the outside steps and rapped on the door. Hank opened it, and a cool blast of air reached out and beckoned Diego inside.

"Come in out of the sun," Hank said. "Man, it's hotter'n Hades out there today. Still no sign of Jessica." He nodded toward the distance.

"I'm beginning to worry." Diego looked at his watch. "She should have been back hours ago." He glanced toward the barn, then back to the house. "I think I'll saddle up, ride out a little way."

Hank picked up a pair of binoculars and held them up to his eyes, turning toward the east.

"What is it?"

"Saw something move, a rider, maybe." Seeing Diego's restlessness, Hank handed him the glasses. "Out there, just beyond that line of sagebrush. See it?"

"Yeah, I see it, but . . ." Diego held his breath

as the horse came into view. It didn't seem to be
in any hurry, and there was something odd about
the look of it. When it came closer, Diego made
a quiet noise and handed the binoculars back to
Hank.

"It's Cowpoke." Diego turned to the door. "The
saddle's empty."

"What?" You sure?" Hank stared hard through
the field glasses. But Diego was out the door and
running down the steps and through the gate.

"Oh, Lord," Hank muttered, slowly lowering the
binoculars and watching Diego sprint across the
dry ground, little spurts of dust flying off his heels
as he ran toward the riderless horse.

Hank leaned out the door. "Eb," he shouted.
"Have someone saddle a horse for Diego. He'll be
riding out soon as he brings Miss Jessica's horse
in. Call the kitchen and have someone throw together some grub for him, too."

When Diego pulled Cowpoke into the barn, another horse was being saddled. One of the men
brought a bag of food and tied it across the saddle. They rubbed down Cowpoke and gave the
horse water and some feed while Diego waited. He
would take the horse with him, hoping somehow
it might lead him back to Jessica.

Within minutes, Diego was riding out of the
barn. He knew Hank was probably the one responsible for anticipating his needs and he waved toward him in the tower.

"Thanks, Hank," he shouted. "Call the house

and tell Mr. McLean what's happened. And tell him not to worry—I'll find her."

For the first few miles, he let Cowpoke take the lead, not tying him or trying to steer him in one direction or another. It soon became apparent where he was heading—toward the stream and the cottonwoods.

"Jess," Diego whispered. "I should have known it was where you'd go." She had taken him there the first time and told him it was where she always went when she was sad or troubled, the one place where she always found peace and solace.

It quickly became *their* place. And it was where, finally, they made love the first time, and many times afterward. That was the reason he had avoided it yesterday on the picnic. He wasn't sure how Jessica would react. To tell the truth, he hadn't been ready to return there himself.

The sagebrush and small trees along the way cast long shadows across the earth as the sun sank lower on the horizon. Overhead the sky turned a deep purple with long streaks of gold and pink in the west. Sometimes out here in the desert, night could fall like a stone, shutting out everything and enclosing the world in total darkness in a matter of minutes.

Diego came into the area from the east side of the stream, and at this point Cowpoke faltered, not wanting to go any further. As he scanned the ground and countryside around him, he saw fresh tracks along the creek and he knew it had to be the horse's earlier trail. He tied Jessica's horse behind him and headed across the stream.

It had been a long time since Diego had been here. Coming in from this side, he wasn't sure where the cottonwoods were. He climbed down from the saddle so he could see Cowpoke's earlier tracks in the gathering darkness. He grabbed his horse's reins and led him and Cowpoke.

By now it was almost completely dark. He thought he smelled smoke and stopped for a moment, gazing through the trees across the stream. He saw a small glimmer of light.

"A campfire." Joy sprang up within him. If Jessica could build a fire, she wasn't hurt badly. He reached out and stroked Cowpoke's nose.

"Let's go."

Diego crossed the stream, pulling the horses behind him.

They crashed through the brush and as they neared the campfire, Diego heard Jessica call out.

Thank God.

At the campfire, Jessica heard a noise. At first her heart almost stopped. What would she do if the cougar whose tracks she'd seen earlier came here to drink?

Then she heard the soft whinny of a horse and she wanted to laugh and cry at the same time. The relief that flooded over her left her weak and limp, but she managed to push herself to her feet.

Earlier she'd removed her boot because her ankle had swollen.

A horse crashed through the underbrush and appeared in the reach of the firelight.

"Cowpoke! Pokey, you big beautiful boy, you came back for me!"

"With just a little help." Diego stepped into the light of the flickering fire.

"Diego!"

In one quick moment, his gaze took in the entire situation. He saw the limb she'd made into a crutch, saw her bare foot, held above the ground. He was so relieved to see her alive and well that his first instinct was to run to her, pull her into his arms, and rain kisses all over her beautiful face.

But after the way they'd parted last night, he was sure Jessica would have none of that.

Instead he held himself back, as if this were the most normal situation in the world, as if he hadn't been frightened out of his wits. He tied his horse to a nearby tree and took out the bag of food before walking into her camp.

Jessica could hardly believe her eyes when she saw him moving toward her. He looked tired and hot. His boots and jeans were wet where he'd crossed the creek, and his denim shirt was streaked with sweat and dust.

He was the most beautiful sight in the world.

"Are you all right?" He stopped, still almost fifty feet away.

"I'm fine." She explained quickly about Cowpoke being spooked by the katydid and how she'd tried to jump away from him. "It's just a sprain."

Today, stranded out here alone, Jessica'd had plenty of time, most of which she'd spent thinking about Diego. And of course, under the cotton-woods, she couldn't help remembering the first time they'd made love. She had been overwhelmed by the physical aspect of lovemaking and even more overwhelmed by the emotions she felt for Diego.

And now here he was again, as if the past were repeating itself. He walked toward her with a look of quiet relief and joy in his beautiful eyes.

God, but she loved him. And seeing him now, she forgot last night and the way she'd been so hurt. She forgot about that morning, when she'd left the house desperate to be alone.

Their eyes met and held as he came toward her. When he was closer, she lifted her arms, letting the walking stick fall away from her. She saw the look of surprise in his eyes as she hobbled toward him and fell into his arms.

Diego dropped the bag he was carrying and gave a quiet groan as his arms went around Jessica. He pulled her against him, his hands tangling in her hair as he kissed her. Her mouth was hot, desper-ate against his, and it sent his senses reeling.

When they finally pulled apart, both of them were breathless.

"Woman," he muttered, looking into her shin-ing eyes, "you had me out of my mind with worry."

"Don't fuss at me," she said, half serious and half teasing.

"I don't mean to, but—"

"Shhh." She lifted her mouth to his once again. "This is so good. *You're* so good," she said, her breath warm against his lips. "I don't want to think about anything else." His rejection of yesterday was forgotten in the moment. All she could think of was the feel of him, the taste of his mouth on hers.

Diego pulled away and held her at arm's length, looking into her eyes. His expression was solemn and puzzled.

"I'll be damned. You're as changeable as the weather."

"I've been alone all day," she said, "and I've had plenty of time to think."

It took all the strength he possessed to pull away from her. He wanted her so desperately it was all he could do not to gather her close and kiss her until they were past caring about where they were or what they were doing—just as they'd been that summer when they couldn't get enough of each other. One touch could set off a storm in them that nothing could stop except the feel of their bodies together and whispered hot, erotic words.

"Sit." He motioned her back to the tree. "I've brought food and water."

Jessica was starving, and the simple meal of cheese and freshly baked bread with some of Cook's homemade pickles was the best thing she'd tasted in ages. While she ate, Diego sat across the fire from her, watching her with a slight grin on his face.

He couldn't believe how she had greeted him. Her kisses still burned against his lips, and he still felt the imprint of her body against his. But where was this heading? And considering the volatility of their relationship since he'd learned about Tommy, was it wise for either of them?

"You're staring, Mr. Serrat." Jessica gave him a teasing grin. She drank from the bottled water, watching him all the while.

"You're beautiful," he said, his eyes dark and warm. "What man wouldn't stare?" He glanced around at the place where they were. "Even more beautiful than you were before."

Her voice dropped shyly. "I've thought about so many things today. This place meant so much to us. We were so trusting then. There was no man in the world I trusted as much as you."

"I know," he said, his voice quiet and thoughtful. "That's one of the things that bothered me the most, losing your trust. I saw it in your eyes when I came back, and I didn't understand."

"I know I've hurt you, but none of it was your fault. Or mine." She started to move toward him, then stopped when she saw his warning look. "What?"

He shook his head. "I've changed, Jessica. I'm not the same person I used to be. And not all of it has to do with us, or you, or what happened with your father."

"What do you mean?" She could feel her pulse

beating in her temples and for a moment, not knowing what he meant, she felt frightened. Was he telling her good-bye?

She had assumed he was here because he had reached the same conclusion as she, that they still belonged together.

"Part of it is my job, I guess—the nature of it. I've seen things I can't even talk about . . . met some of the lowest people God ever put on earth. That changes a man, Jess. I had to learn not to trust anyone except myself. And now it isn't easy to let someone in again."

"I don't care about all that. We can fix that with a little time. But I want you, Diego. I've never wanted any other man."

He shook his head, his expression filled with sadness and regret.

"Everything can be different this time." She didn't want to sound pleading, but it was the way she felt.

"Don't, Jess." He picked up a leaf, fiddling with it until he looked up and across at her. "Don't make promises you can't keep. The boy and girl who made love here are gone. No matter how much we want it, no matter how hard we try, we may never be able to bring them back."

"You're afraid."

He let out a short bark of laughter. "Damned right I'm afraid."

Her earlier elation left her. He was right. She was always the impulsive, optimistic one, the one willing to jump in and assume everything would be all right. But it hadn't been all right. And the physical passion that still burned brightly between them was no guarantee their lives would ever be all right again. She couldn't blame him for being cautious before reaching out toward the flame that had burned him once before.

Neither of them could be certain about the future, except that Tommy would be in it for both of them. Jessica could hardly bear to think that would be all. She wanted more, so much more. She wanted it all—Tommy and Diego, a family. But she didn't say that. She couldn't until she knew for certain he wanted it, too.

"I understand," she said quietly.

"I'm sorry, Jess."

Jessica stood up, reaching out for him, her attempt at a smile weak and tremulous. "Help me to my horse. Everyone will be worried to death if we don't get back tonight."

"Jess," he said, his voice husky with emotion.

"No, I mean it. I do understand. Really, it's all right." She looked tenderly into his eyes. Then she put her arm out and he came to his feet, stepping to her and putting his arm around her. "Whatever happens, I know it will be all right."

Diego said nothing. He wasn't so certain. He just stood there, looking at her with the darkness of the world in his eyes.

FOURTEEN

The next morning Jessica tried not to be depressed. Instead she tried to focus on Diego's sweetness when he'd brought her home last night and the soft kiss he placed on her lips when he'd said good night.

After she'd showered and put on pajamas, he was waiting with aspirin, an ice pack, and sweet sympathy.

This morning she felt like hell. She probably looked worse after a terrible night of tossing and turning and trying to find a comfortable place for her ankle. The one bright spot was that the rest and ice pack had definitely helped. Her ankle was much better.

She was glad it was the first of the month. That meant she had a lot of work to do, from ordering supplies and paying bills to making out payroll for the ranch hands.

The ranch was a big operation. Sometimes when she felt overwhelmed by the responsibilities, her father would urge her to hire someone to help. At certain times of the year, such as roundup time, she would relent and call one of the temp agencies in town.

In reality, she liked it just the way it was today, with no one else in the cozy office. And today, needing to find a distraction from Diego, she was glad she had so much to keep her busy.

Knowing she needed to be comfortable today, she dressed in a pair of worn, faded jeans and an oversized denim shirt. She slipped into a pair of sandals that wouldn't bother her ankle, then ran a brush quickly and carelessly through her hair, leaving it loose. She didn't bother with makeup at all.

Rosie and Sheila would entertain Tommy today while she worked.

Jessica grabbed a croissant and cup of hot chocolate and headed for her office. Normally she might speak to her father, but this morning he was out at the barn, buying new calves for the season.

She'd been working steadily most of the morning when she heard a knock at the door.

"Come in," she said, barely looking up.

Rosie came in and placed a small square brown package on the corner of the desk.

"Delivery for you, Jessica."

"What is it?" Jessica asked, waving a pencil toward the package.

"I have no idea. But Diego was not at all pleased about me bringing it in to you. He wanted me to give it to him."

"Why?" Jessica put down her pen and sat back in her chair.

"I'll tell you why." Diego stalked into the room, looking tanned and full of energy. Somehow he didn't seem as sweet and solicitous as he had last night.

Oddly, he carried a large bucket, something that puzzled Jessica.

"I gave orders that any mail or unexpected packages were to go through me. Perhaps that's something you forgot to tell the rest of the household." His glance at Rosie was withering.

Rosie grimaced and lifted her brows. She sidled across the room, slipping behind Diego. With a sheepish little wave at Jessica, she hurried out the door.

Jessica sighed. "What is this all about? I have work to do and I don't have time for—"

Without warning, Diego scooped up the package that lay on the desk and plopped it into the bucket, splashing water out on the carpet.

Jessica jumped up from her chair, groaning at the pain in her ankle. She stared at him as if he'd lost his mind.

"What on earth are you doing?" she shouted.

"This package has no return address." Diego's brows were furrowed with determination. "The address is practically unreadable and"—he paused for emphasis—"it's making a noise."

"Oh, for goodness sake. Aren't you being overdramatic? Here." Jessica hurried around the desk, reaching for the soaking package. "Give me that."

"Not until I get it outside and make sure it's safe." He pulled the bucket out of her reach.

"You're being an idiot about this. Don't you think dumping my package into a bucket of water is going a bit too far, even for you?"

"Do you have any idea who sent it?" he asked smugly.

She frowned, staring down at the wet brown package. She couldn't remember ordering anything.

Then she saw a red wax seal on the back and she shook her head. When she looked up into his eyes, there was a wry, self-satisfied smile on her lips.

"As a matter of fact, I think I do." She practically purred. "If I'm not mistaken, that little red seal on the back tells me it came from a very old Chinese gentleman who runs an antique store in El Paso. If his handwriting is illegible, it's because he barely learned to read or write English. I've had a standing order with him for this antique Chinese clock—oh, my Lord!" she exclaimed. "My clock! You've ruined my clock!"

"There's no return address," Diego insisted, his confidence not wavering one inch. He held the package out of her reach.

"Will you give me that?" She grabbed for it and found herself trapped against his hard chest. His one arm held her against him. His other held the bucket and its contents away from her.

"It's ticking."

"Of course it's ticking. It's an antique clock.

Priceless, I might add—or it was until you drowned it."

He pulled away and went around her, carrying the bucket out a side door and onto a small patio.

Jessica followed, not sure if she should laugh or cry when she saw him reach down into the water to poke at the soaking package with an ink pen.

"That should do it." He threw a look of smug satisfaction over his shoulder.

"Oh, that should do it all right," she said dryly, "if total destruction is your goal. You've lost your mind."

Carefully he slipped the wrapping off the package, using the tip of his pen. "I don't see any wires."

Jessica rolled her eyes and shook her head. "Of course there are no wires."

"Can't be too careful," he muttered, fiercely intent on his purpose.

When the wet wrapping lay on the stone patio, Diego lifted the bubble-wrapped item and put it on the ground.

Jessica stood back, her arms across her chest as she watched him. As each layer of packing was removed and the clock became visible, she began to grin broadly.

"Boom," she said quietly.

"Very funny." His look of amused chagrin acknowledged his mistake.

He stood up, holding the dripping clock gingerly in front of him. He glowered at Jessica as he pulled a clean white handkerchief from his pocket and began wiping the clock dry.

"If you'd listened to me," he scolded, "this wouldn't have happened."

"Oh, now it's my fault that you've ruined my clock?"

"I told you specifically you would have to do everything I said. You do remember that, don't you? In the hallway the other day, you said you had no problem with my being in charge."

"I can't believe I'd ever say such a thing." She tried to keep from laughing.

"Woman," he muttered, "you are trying my patience."

"OK, OK, from now on, I'll make sure all packages and all mail come through you, oh great one. Satisfied?"

He continued to glower at her beneath dark, furrowed brows. "There." He handed the clock to her. "Good as new."

Just then the little blue and white clock began to chime, making a decidedly sick little sound in the still morning air.

"Uh-huh, good as new." Jessica giggled, then covered her mouth. But it was no good. In a second she found herself laughing almost hysterically, bending over and holding her stomach.

"Ohhh," she said. "I'm sorry. Really . . ."

"You're not sorry. You're enjoying this."

"You're right, I am. The look on your face when you pulled that pitiful little clock out of there—oh, I'll never forget it."

"It's downright disrespectful, laughing at a dedicated law enforcement officer trying to do his duty."

But despite his words, Diego was grinning broadly. Then he, too, began to chuckle, finally laughing as hard as she was.

Jessica regained control of herself first and plopped down onto one of the patio chairs, holding the clock up to her ear to hear it ticking.

"I love this little clock," she said. "I'm glad you didn't drown it, although you did give it the old Ranger try."

Diego pointed his finger at her, then sat down in a chair across from her, sighing with pleasure and good humor. He leaned back in the chair and clasped his hands behind his head, studying her.

"By the way, how's your ankle?"

"It's much better, thank you."

"I'm glad." They sat for a moment, not speaking. "It's good to hear you laugh again." His eyes changed and his voice suddenly turned serious.

Jessica was still smiling and her eyes sparkled when she answered him. "It's good to hear you laugh, too."

Diego thought he'd never seen her look more beautiful. He liked her hair loose the way it was today. In her faded jeans and with no makeup, she looked like a teenager.

"You look great today. Sexy as hell, actually."

Jessica frowned, disconcerted by his admiring look, especially after last night. His gaze didn't

miss a thing, from her head down to her painted
pink toenails.

"I . . . I like being comfortable when I'm working."

"Whatever it is," he said, "you should keep doing it."

They sat for a few moments in almost companionable silence, enjoying the morning breeze and
the scent of flowers that wafted toward them from
the gardens.

"Jessica, about last night—"

"Please, if we talk about that, you and I will spoil
this perfectly lovely day." They both grinned.
"Let's just let it be for a while and see what happens."

Diego knew what he wanted to happen, but he
didn't say it. He pursed his lips, knowing that stubborn look on her face. She was near the point of
shutting him out again. He didn't want their
shared laughter to end in another argument.

"All right." He shrugged his broad shoulders.

He stood up and walked to her. Cupping her
chin in his hand, he forced her to look up at him.
Then he left and she sat looking wistfully at the
little blue willow clock.

So many feelings warred inside of her, not least
the way she felt when he was around. She wanted
him. Desperately.

She wanted him at this very moment. Sometimes
she wondered what he would do if she went to
him, wherever he was, and told him, if she

reached out for him and whispered all the things she wanted . . . needed.

Jessica closed her eyes at the thought, holding her breath, aware of the soft breeze against her skin. She was aware of the smallest senses today, as if her body had grown keenly attuned to the air around her. For a moment she could still feel the touch of his hand on her cheek.

It wasn't over between them. If she had anything to do with it, it never would be.

FIFTEEN

Jessica had a late lunch in her office, and by the time she finished work, it was well past supper. Not that it mattered; she wasn't that hungry. But she was anxious to see Tommy. She had barely seen him all day.

She hurried upstairs, finding the house especially quiet this evening. She couldn't help wondering where Diego was. She hadn't seen him, either, since the episode with the clock.

The remembrance of that had kept her smiling all day.

She was just going down the hall toward her room when she heard her father's voice behind her.

"Jessica."

She turned and saw him with Tommy, hand in hand.

"Well," she said. "What are you two up to?"

"I'm spending the night with grandpa." Tommy's eyes were bright and sparkling. "We're going to watch movies and eat popcorn."

"Really? That sounds like fun. What's showing tonight? I might join you."

"Oh, I don't think you want to do that." Her father's look was mysterious, but filled with good humor. He grinned and nodded toward her room.

"Why don't you go on inside? You'll see what I mean." He pulled at Tommy's hand. "Come on, bud. Tell your mommy good night."

"Night, Mom," Tommy said, turning and waving.

Jessica stood in the hallway for a moment, then turned slowly and pushed open the door to her room.

Everything seemed in place. She didn't notice anything unusual until she caught a glimpse of color on the bed.

A beautiful mint green dress was spread across the coverlet. Frowning, she touched the material and glanced around the room.

"What in the world?" she wondered aloud.

"I'm pretty sure it's your size."

She turned to see Diego leaning against the woodwork in the doorway between their rooms. He was wearing a pair of cream-colored slacks and a black dinner jacket.

Her eyes moved over him in wide disbelief. She wasn't sure she'd ever seen him wearing anything except jeans. But tonight, dressed formally, he took her breath away.

"What are you doing?" she asked, a quiet smile flickering across her lips.

"Inviting you to dinner." He didn't move from his position in the doorway.

"But I . . ."

"In the courtyard."

Jessica was amazed and speechless. She had grown used to Diego's disciplined, take-charge side, but she'd never seen this engaging, completely sophisticated side.

"Well?" He smiled at her hesitation and obvious amazement. "Are you going to get dressed? Or shall I come in and help you?"

"No," she said, her smile soft and flirtatious. "No, I think I can manage to dress myself. Give me a few minutes."

He glanced at his watch, then back at her.

"In fifteen minutes, I'll knock on your patio door."

Her lips parted and she could only stare at him, not knowing what to say or what to make of this new Diego.

He turned and softly closed the door without saying another word, but not before she saw the look on his face. He knew he had stunned her, and he was enjoying every minute of it.

So was she.

After a quick shower, Jessica slipped the green dress over her head, letting it fall in luscious perfection almost to the floor. The silk lining beneath the lacy material felt smooth and erotic against her skin. When she turned to look in the mirror, she could hardly believe it was her reflection.

The scooped neckline was held up by tiny straps. The rest of the dress, a soft A-line, fit well across her breasts, then fell softly over her hips and thighs. She smoothed her hands over the material, delighting in the new rich smell of it.

How long had it been since she'd worn a dress like this, since she'd felt enough interest in how she looked to want a dress like this?

She'd just slipped on a pair of strappy little heels when Diego knocked at the patio door. Jessica actually felt shy going to the door and opening it. He was so elegant, so handsome. For a moment she felt like the high-school wallflower being escorted by the best looking guy in school. But as soon as she saw the look in his eyes, her confidence returned.

"Wow." He made no effort to hide what he was feeling as he let his eyes move slowly, admiringly over her and back up to her face. "I'd have said it was impossible."

"What?" she asked, her voice soft.

"That you could look even more beautiful than you were on another night when I took you to a dance and you wore a green dress."

Jessica cocked her head to one side, blinking her eyes and looking down at the dress again. "I'd completely forgotten that. But now that you mention it, this one is very much like it. I'm surprised you remember."

"Lady, I haven't forgotten a thing where you're concerned."

"But where did you . . . how did you—"

"From a catalog, via the computer. I ordered it this morning, they delivered it this afternoon. And this time, thank goodness, no one dumped the package into a bucket of water."

"How did you manage all this without my knowing? I met my father in the hallway. I take it he knew all about it, but I can hardly believe he was your ally."

"Believe it," he said, with feigned innocence. "When I told him what I wanted to do, he was all for it. He even volunteered to keep Tommy all night."

Jessica's eyes changed and she looked away from his steady gaze.

"No, wait, it isn't that. I didn't make plans for us to be alone so I could . . ." He shook his head. For a moment, he actually seemed at a loss for words. "Not that the thought hadn't crossed my mind," he added with a quick grin. "But I thought it might be easier to talk if we were alone. Kind of like starting all over again, getting to know one another. Getting to know the people we are today."

"Sounds good." Jessica's head was still spinning.

"Look, I know I've been doing this all wrong, and the other night proved it to me. I don't want to make you cry, Jess. You don't deserve to have me come here to your home and make you so unhappy."

His words and the sincerity with which he said them made her heart so full of love, she thought she would burst. At that moment, if he had said the real purpose for Tommy's staying with his grandfather was to get her into bed, she wouldn't have objected in the least.

But the fact that he wanted to take the time to get to know her again, to know her needs and

what she wanted, filled her with more love than
anything he could have done.

"What about Tommy?" She didn't trust herself
to ask anything more personal. "What did he
think?"

"Oh, I didn't even try to explain it to him. He's
too young to understand, and the last thing I want
to do is confuse him."

Jessica laughed and Diego stepped forward,
holding out his arm to her. She slipped her hand
around his arm, holding on tightly and looking
up into his eyes. "You constantly surprise me."

"Good." He led her out onto the balcony and
down into the courtyard.

Music played somewhere in the background,
very soft Spanish guitars and violins, a combina-
tion that made her sigh with pleasure.

"This is wonderful," she whispered.

He led her to the center of the courtyard near
a fountain that sprinkled down fine showers of
water. Nearby was a small table covered with a
linen cloth. Tall wrought-iron candleholders had
been placed all around the table. Massed together
as they were, they lit the area brightly. The flames
flickered in the wind, throwing little shadows
across the table and illuminating the dinnerware
and crystal with starry sparkles.

"Oh, my." She touched her hand to her throat
in awe and disbelief.

She turned to him. He watched her, his eyes in
the candle glow dark and mysterious and more

beautiful than she'd ever dreamed. "I . . . I don't know what to say."

"You don't have to say anything." He pulled out a chair for her. "I just want you to enjoy the evening. It's my way of apologizing for the Chinese clock."

She might have been disappointed if she hadn't already seen the look in his eyes. She had no doubt he felt bad about the clock, but she knew he wanted to be here with her as much as she wanted it.

"The clock is happily ticking away in my office at this very moment," she said, "none the worse for wear."

"I'm glad to hear it." He took his seat across from her.

He removed a bottle of champagne from a silver cooler and filled her glass, then his.

"I'd like to make a toast." He held his glass forward.

Jessica picked up her champagne glass and lifted it toward his.

"To a new beginning," he said.

His eyes held a certain regret and his words, said so softly, so sincerely, sent a pang of tenderness through Jessica. Her chin trembled slightly, but she managed to smile and nod her agreement.

"Jessica, I've handled this all wrong. And it isn't what I want, the fighting, the misunderstandings, the crying. God, I never could stand to see you cry."

"I'm sorry about that. I—"

"No, don't," he said. "It was my fault completely. I gave Tommy my word and I shouldn't have broken it. I'm too hard sometimes. I know I am. But it isn't the way I want to be with Tommy, and certainly not with you."

Jessica hardly knew what to say. She couldn't believe what she was hearing, or the way he was looking at her.

"What do you say? Do you think it's possible to forget the past, to move beyond all the hurts and the blame? God knows there's enough of that to go around, but rehashing it every day isn't going to change anything."

"I agree. Not that I'm sure I deserve it." She lifted her glass to his and took a small sip.

"I don't want to hear you say that again. You do deserve it. And so do I. There's nothing wrong with wanting to be happy."

"But I need to know something, Diego. What exactly does this mean? Are we to be friends?"

"I hope so," he said solemnly. "And more," he added, his eyes growing dark.

"I guess 'more' is the part I'm asking about." Her voice was almost a whisper.

"We both know how we feel. There's no denying that I want you. I don't think I've ever . . ." He took a deep breath, as if trying to regain his composure. When he spoke again, his words were slower and more carefully chosen. "Maybe we're putting the cart before the horse." He groaned slightly and grinned at her. "I can't believe I'm saying this, that I'm advocating slowing everything down."

"Go on," she whispered. "You're doing fine."

"Maybe, like you said, this time we should get to know one another first." He lifted his palms in a gesture of explanation.

"Maybe so." She sipped her champagne and gazed at him over the rim of the glass.

"If you keep looking at me that way," he growled, "I'm going to ruin this whole selfless act I've got going here by leaping over the table and—"

Jessica laughed softly and placed her glass on the table.

"I don't mean to be a temptation," she said demurely.

"Liar."

Both of them laughed and he reached across the table. Jessica looked into his eyes and took his hand.

"Do you think we can do this?"

"For Tommy, we can do anything." She didn't want to risk ruining everything, but she had to know who he was doing this for.

"For Tommy," he agreed, nodding seriously. "But for us, too, Jess. And I'll be honest, I have no idea where it's going. We might still end up apart. Hell, we might even end up hating each other."

"I doubt that."

His responding smile warmed her clear down to her toes.

"But I do want us to try. When this is all over, I don't want to go back to Austin and spend the rest of my life wondering what might have happened if only I'd given it another chance."

"Talk about leaping across the table," she murmured, letting him know how much she wanted him.

He laughed, and for a moment the look in his eyes was so intense, she thought he might get up and come around to her. Instead he took a deep breath and shook his finger at her. "Woman, you are killing me."

"Then perhaps we should stop talking and have dinner," she suggested with a pleased laugh.

"I think you're right." He stood up and walked past the barrier of candles, waving toward someone in the darkness.

Within seconds, their dinner was delivered—prime rib, still warm and succulent, and fresh asparagus, her favorite, along with oven-roasted potatoes.

She hadn't enjoyed a meal since Diego had returned. But tonight, her appetite and her enjoyment were back, and she wanted to shout to the world how happy she was.

Only because of his words could she make herself remain silent and outwardly cool. Inside, she was on fire.

She loved him. Perhaps she'd never stopped loving him, even through the bad times. For the first time in years, she could admit that to herself. She loved him more than ever, and she wanted him back in her life to stay.

But she dared not say it, dared not even think it until this was all over and they were safe.

After they ate, they sat talking quietly, chatting about everyday things and funny moments they remembered. They laughed about Tommy and his antics. Then the courtyard grew quiet and there was only the sound of Spanish guitars in the background blending with cricket sounds and the soft water murmuring in the fountain.

"I can't remember enjoying an evening more."

"Neither can I." Diego reached across the table, palm upward, and she placed her hand in his.

"Do you think it's safe for us to dance?" he asked, his eyes twinkling mischievously.

"I feel perfectly safe. How about you?"

"Safe is not what I feel when I'm with you." He came around, pulling her to her feet and into his arms. "To hell with safety."

He held her close and Jessica nuzzled her face against his neck, breathing in the sexy scent of him. They fit so well together, as if they were made for one another.

When the music stopped, Jessica didn't want it to end, and she didn't want to leave the warmth of his strong arms.

She could see he wasn't ready for it to end, either.

"Diego, I have to tell you something—just this one last time. Then I swear I won't bring it up again until you want to talk about it."

He pulled back, his arms still around her, still swaying slowly as they waited for the next song.

"Sounds awfully serious."

"It is. Diego, I'm so sorry for what I did. I knew as soon as Tommy was born that I should get in touch with you. But I was angry and stubborn and hateful. It was the biggest mistake I've ever made, and I'll regret it the rest of my life. Seeing you again, knowing it wasn't your fault, every time I think about it I have this sick, terrible feeling inside."

He took a deep breath and she could feel the tension in his arms and chest.

"I know you mean that. And I'm trying, Jess. I swear, I'm trying."

"I want you to forgive me," she whispered. "I know it's asking a lot, but right now, right here, with this new beginning before us, I'm asking you to please try to forgive me for the wrong I've done you."

Her eyes in the candlelight sparkled with unshed tears.

"I'm begging you to see it had nothing to do with who you are or who you family was. I'll admit I never fully understood the anguish you suffered as a boy, but I knew it bothered you and it only made me love you more. You're a good man, Diego Serrat, a proud and noble man any woman would be blessed to have in her life. I'm proud of Tommy, and I'm doubly proud you're his father."

Her voice faded to a whisper as she struggled to get the words out.

For long moments he was silent. Then, just when she was convinced he would turn away from her, he pulled her hand to his mouth, placing a soft kiss against her skin that caused a rush of weakness to wash over her.

"I want you to know this. I'm not deliberately holding onto any resentments or regrets. I want to put all that behind me. I do. And I swear to you tonight, here in this beautiful place, I'll try with all my heart. I know that doesn't sound like much but I—"

"No, it sounds fine." She placed her fingers against his lips. "It's enough. It's all I ask, that you give me a chance."

SIXTEEN

Diego escorted Jessica back to her room, telling her good night at the door with a sweet but chaste kiss that left her wanting more.

When he groaned and made a pretense of pulling himself away, Jessica laughed. She was still laughing when she went inside and closed the door.

She undressed, placing the dress on a hanger over the edge of the closet door. She didn't want to put it away yet. Later, just before getting into bed, she walked to where the dress hung, took the material in her hands and lifted it to her face, certain the scent of Diego's sexy aftershave lingered in the frothy material.

After the lights were out, she lay in bed for a long while, staring at the dim outline of the dress and reliving every word, every look, every moment of the evening.

She still had a lot of work to, and the next morning she rose early, stopping by the dining room for coffee.

Rosie was clearing the table.

"Diego just left. Said to tell you he'd be back around noon and he'd like to have lunch with you and Tommy."

"Oh." Jessica smiled to herself, not yet willing to say anything about last night. The truce between her and Diego was still too new and much too fragile to talk about.

"Tommy's still with Dad?"

"He's still sleeping. They must have stayed up half the night watching their movies."

Jessica stepped to the windows for a moment, gazing out at the hazy purple mountains in the distance.

"Oh, Rosie, isn't it a perfectly beautiful day?" She stretched her arms above her head and sighed with pure pleasure.

"Well, looks like something's put you in a good mood. Might it have anything to do with the dinner I hear was catered in the courtyard last night?"

"It might." Jessica laughed and took a sip of her coffee. "It just might."

She found herself distracted all day. She couldn't seem to think of anything except the previous night and the look in Diego's eyes.

Though she warned herself not to become too hopeful, she found herself daydreaming, thinking of a life somewhere with Diego and their son.

She could hardly wait until lunch. When she walked into the dining room and saw Diego waiting for her, she thought her heart might actually stop.

He and Tommy were at the large windows with her father, looking out at the scenery. Her father turned and motioned her into the room.

"Come join us, honey. We're just looking at the mountains. Diego was telling Tommy about all the great hunting and fishing places up there."

"He's going to take me there one day, Mom."

"Oh, is he?" She thought she'd never seen such wonder as there was on her son's face that day. "That sounds like fun."

She looked up at Diego. The smile he gave her was special, and she knew he was remembering the previous night, too. For a moment it was as if there were only the two of them in the room.

"I told Grandpa that Diego's my dad." Tommy's voice was filled with pride, as if he had just done something magnificent. His statement, made so matter-of-factly, astonished Jessica, coming as it did from a four year old.

"He said he already knew it," Tommy added, his eyes wide.

Diego's teeth tugged at his lower lip. She could see he was trying valiantly not to lose his composure.

Jessica eyed her father. "And what did Grandpa think about that?"

"He likes it. He'll probably go with us when me and Diego go camping in the mountains. We'll all three be buddies." He turned to look out the window, asking more questions.

Diego laughed out loud, obviously enjoying Frank McLean's look of embarrassment.

Frank muttered something and cleared his throat loudly, looking very serious when he turned Tommy toward the table.

"I think it's high time we had lunch, boy."

"Sure, Grandpa." Tommy scurried to his chair at the table. "You sit here, Diego." He pointed to the chair beside him, where Jessica usually sat.

"That's your mother's chair." Diego glanced over at Jessica.

"No, that's fine." She was so happy she was practically beaming, and she couldn't hide it. "You sit there and I'll sit on the other side. Then we both get to sit next to Tommy."

Tommy was grinning from ear to ear as they all took their seats.

They had just started their meal when Diego's cell phone rang. He didn't bother getting up from the table, but casually pulled the phone out of his pocket.

"Excuse me. Serrat," he said into the phone.

Jessica watched him out of the corner of her eye, and she noticed the quizzical look on his face.

"She's where?" he asked, his voice filled with disbelief. "Here? I'll be right there."

"What?" Jessica was alarmed.

"It's nothing to worry about," he said, disconnecting. But his frown made her wonder. He rubbed his hand down the side of his face, shaking his head in disbelief.

"Is it Colby?" Frank asked. "He hasn't—"

"No, not Colby. Although believe me, I might have preferred that."

"Diego, what is it?"

"It's my mother." He shrugged his broad shoulders. For a moment, he looked like a little boy who was about to receive a lecture. "She's outside at the gates."

"You told her?" Jessica asked.

"Yes, I told her. She has a right to know, doesn't she?"

"Of course she does. I didn't mean that." For a moment Jessica thought the conversation might escalate into another argument of blame and past regrets. But then Diego's look softened and he smiled at her and reached over to take her hand.

"Well, never mind that. Maria is here? That's marvelous." Frank stood up and pushed his chair back. "I'll go see her in. You two stay here and—"

"I don't think you want to do that. Seems she's come to see her grandson, and I have a feeling she's not going to be too happy with any of us. Better let me go."

"I have a grandmother?" Tommy shouted, causing Frank to jump.

"For heaven's sake, boy. Stop yelling."

"Well, do I?" he asked, more quietly.

"Yes, you have a grandmother," Jessica said. "She's a very nice lady and I'm sure she's going to adore you. So you be on your best behavior."

Suddenly her heart was pounding at the thought of Maria Serrat here to see her grandson and to no doubt confront Jessica and Frank McLean about what they had done.

Just when she thought things might actually be getting better. . . .

"It will be OK," Diego said. "Just remember, she doesn't bite," he added softly over his shoulder as he turned to leave the room.

"Did she used to bite?" Tommy asked.

Diego laughed, giving Jessica one last look of encouragement. She could still hear him chuckling as he went out the door.

Jessica couldn't eat another bite of lunch, but Maria Serrat's visit didn't seem to bother her father very much. He and Tommy joked and laughed and continued eating after Jessica left the table and went to stand at the windows.

By the time Diego returned, she had calmed herself only a little.

She faced his mother, knowing full well Maria would resent her as much as Diego had when he first learned about Tommy.

Maria was a small woman. Her sleek black hair, now streaked with gray, was pulled back into a stylish twist. She stood beside Diego as Frank McLean got up and went forward to shake her hand. She seemed friendly enough, but she was obviously distracted by Tommy's presence, although she was making an effort not to overwhelm him.

"And Jessica." Diego nodded toward her.

"Mrs. Serrat," Jessica said, from her position at the window. "We're so pleased you could come." She sounded stiff and formal, but she couldn't seem to help it. She had no idea how to deal with this.

Diego might have gotten his height and muscular build from his father, but his handsome features definitely came from his mother. She had the same high cheekbones, the same dark skin. And right now, she was looking at Jessica with sparkling black eyes that held the same questions Jessica had seen in Diego's.

"Please have lunch with us. I'll get another place setting. Would you like tea? Coffee?" Jessica busied herself at the sideboard, bringing out dishes and silverware.

"Coffee will be fine, thank you." Maria sat down beside Tommy, and her dark eyes grew tender and warm.

"Oh, Diego." She looked up at her tall, handsome son. "He looks so much like you when you were that age."

"Are you my grandmother?"

Maria laughed, obviously delighted Tommy had already been told who she was.

"Why, yes, I am. And I'm very pleased to meet you."

Tommy reached out, almost shyly, his hand closing around Diego's fingers. That small, unexpected gesture brought a sudden lump to Jessica's throat.

"He's my dad," Tommy said, his voice proud.

"Yes, I know. And what did you think about that?" Maria asked.

"I like having a dad."

Diego smiled. Then, touching Tommy's hair, he took his place again at the table.

"Jess," he asked, "are you finished eating? You hardly touched your salad."

"I . . . I'm not very hungry today."

She knew she hadn't fooled him. He knew perfectly well why her appetite had suddenly disappeared. And if the glance from Maria was any indication, so did she.

Somehow they managed to finish the meal without too much awkwardness, partly because of Maria's growing enchantment with her grandson, and partly, Jessica was surprised to see, because of how gracious and welcoming her father was to Maria.

Jessica and Diego glanced at each other often. She was sure he felt as she did. It was an awkward and strange situation.

Rosie brought a plate of freshly baked cookies, but hesitated at the doorway, her eyes wide and filled with surprise.

"Maria?" she said. "I can hardly believe it's really you. It's so good to see you again."

"It's good to see you, too, Rosie." Maria smiled broadly. "I couldn't wait any longer to see my grandson, even though Diego tried to convince me this was not the best time."

"Guess you noticed all the security and the guards," Rosie said.

"Yes." Maria's eyes clouded with worry. But just as quickly, the look was gone as she turned to Tommy. "Tommy, would you like to show your grandmother around the ranch?"

"Sure." Tommy took a cookie from the plate

Rosie held toward him. "We have a new colt and some new calves."

"I'd love to see them," Maria said. "And then later"—her glance moved over Jessica and then Diego—"maybe your mother and I could talk a bit, catch up on all the news."

"We could have tea, if you'd like," Jessica said, relieved that their talk would not be delayed or brushed aside. It was something that needed to be done and over with, and she was anxious to do just that.

"That sounds nice," Maria said with a tight little smile.

"I'll be in my office whenever you're ready. There's a patio just outside where we can sit and talk. I think you'll enjoy it."

"Oh, you must mean your mother's old office." Maria nodded. "It was one of my favorite rooms."

"Yes." Jessica had forgotten Maria knew this house as well as she did. "My mother's old office."

"Let me change my clothes," Maria said to Tommy, "and then we'll go see all your new animals."

"I think I'll tag along, Maria," Frank said, pushing away from the table, "if you don't mind."

"I don't mind at all."

After they were gone, Diego came to Jessica and took her hand, pulling her up from the chair and into his arms.

"Don't look so apprehensive," he whispered. "Everything's going to be fine. I explained the situation to Mother, and she knows how I feel about working things out."

"She's bound to be angry and resentful, and I don't blame her."

"Do you want me to join you for tea to help smooth things over?"

"No," Jessica said. "Not that I wouldn't love it, but this is between your mother and me. I can handle it."

"Just be honest. That's all you can do. And don't worry. She's got a heart as big as Texas, and she always loved you. She's just being a little motherly and protective right now, that's all. Once she's accepted the way things are, she'll be fine."

SEVENTEEN

"The way things are." Jessica repeated Diego's words to herself as she sat on the patio waiting for Mrs. Serrat.

How exactly were things between them? He sounded as if she should know.

But she didn't.

Even after the previous night and feeling as if they might finally be getting somewhere, she still couldn't be sure.

She knew he meant them to be friends and to deal fairly with the sharing of their son. She knew he wanted them to start over, and she knew he wanted her physically. But after a few hours of being away from him, she began to doubt even that.

She was so deep in thought, she was hardly aware when Maria opened the door and stepped out onto the patio.

"Jessica?"

"Oh, hi." Jessica stood up. "You're here." How foolish she sounded, and how completely unnerved. "Please, have a seat. Someone will bring our tea in a moment."

Maria had changed into white pants and a bright yellow shirt that emphasized her striking, dark features. She looked more relaxed, but hardly less intimidating.

"Well." Jessica sat down across the table from Maria. "It must have come as quite a shock to you, learning about Tommy."

"Quite a shock, yes." Maria nodded. She was watching Jessica, her eyes shrewd and thoughtful. "You know, Jessica, I've never been one to mince words, and I'm not about to start now. So I'll just get right to the point."

"I don't blame you if you hate me."

"I didn't say I hate you. And never mind my feelings in all this." Maria frowned and made a noise of impatience through her teeth. "For heaven's sake, child, I've known you since you were a little girl. But I swear, I don't think I even remotely know the person who could have done such a thing to my son. Four years! Four years you kept his child from him. How could you have done that? That's all I want to know. I'm sure you must have had your reasons, and I'd like to know what they are."

"Did . . . did Diego tell you anything? About my father and what he did?"

"Are you trying to say this is Frank's fault?"

"No, not entirely," Jessica said, her tone firmer.

"All Diego would tell me was that there had been a terrible misunderstanding when he left here. He said he didn't have time to get into all of that on the phone." Maria shrugged her shoulders. "Why do you think I came? I couldn't stand another minute of not knowing. Call me a nosy mother if you want, but—"

"I understand why you came, and I understand your need to know what's going on. Actually, I'm glad you came. The sooner we get this out in the open, the better it will be for all of us."

Jessica's words seemed to calm Maria a bit, and she sat back in her chair, seeming a little more patient.

One of the girls brought a tray of tea and a plate of sandwiches and small decorated cakes. Jessica smiled weakly and waited until she was gone before pouring two cups of tea.

Maria helped herself to the goodies.

"My, these look wonderful," she murmured, almost to herself. "Who is your cook now?" Then, with an amused smile at herself, she waved her fingers in the air. "Never mind. First things first. You were saying?"

Jessica couldn't help smiling, too. Maria never hid the fact that she enjoyed food. It was one of the reasons she loved to cook, she'd often said.

Jessica told Maria what her father had done and how Diego had left without an explanation. The story spilled out of her and from time to time, she had to stop and compose herself when she became too emotional.

"I was wrong," she said when she finished. "I knew I was wrong long ago, before Diego ever came back and discovered for himself the terrible secret I'd been keeping. But I just . . . I just couldn't bring myself . . . I was so afraid and I just didn't know what to do."

"And if Diego had never come back," Maria asked, her voice hard and unforgiving, "would he ever have known about Tommy? Perhaps you planned on sending him an invitation to his son's college graduation?"

Jessica clamped her lips together and swallowed hard. Maria's sarcasm hurt, but she deserved it and more.

"I'm sorry," Jessica whispered. "I'm truly sorry. Seeing Diego and now you, I can't believe what I did. I was so wrong and I'm sorry. I wish you could forgive me, but I'll understand if you can't."

Maria stared at Jessica, her dark eyes hard and troubled. But when she spoke, her voice was softer than it had been.

"Jessica, you were always a good girl. Sweet and loving and just an all-around good girl. But a child can't learn what she isn't taught. I know how hard you tried to please your father. He was a cold man—completely selfish, as far as I was concerned. He says he's changed. Has he?"

"Yes, I think he has. After Mother died, he did change quite a bit; even more after Tommy was born."

"Your mother was a kind woman. I'm sure all of this was very hard on her."

"She wanted me to tell Diego. Even my father, after a while, thought I should. But by then it had gone too far. I had fallen into this pattern of deceit, and I didn't know how to get out."

"Oh, Jessica." Maria shook her head sadly. "I can see how much this has hurt you. How it still hurts you. And I'd have to be blind not to see that my son is ready to move on. Ready to forgive you, even."

"I'm not so sure about that," Jessica said, remembering Diego's words the previous evening.

"I know my son," Maria said, her voice soft. "Outwardly he can seem hard—even cruel sometimes. But that's all a facade that he's erected over the years partly because of his job and partly, I suspect, because of the way he grew up." Maria looked down at her hands. "I blame myself for a lot of that. So you see, everyone in life has some kind of guilt to bear."

"You were a wonderful mother. He loves you very much."

"I know, I know. Inside he has a heart of gold. And he loves Tommy already as if he'd been here with you from the beginning."

"Yes, he does," Jessica agreed. "He doesn't deserve what I did. I promise you, if it takes the rest of my life, I'll try and make it up to him."

"You can't," Maria said, her voice still a bit edgy, "even if you want to. And I believe with all my heart that you do, dear. But you can never make it up. What you have to do . . . what we all have to do . . . is put it behind us and go on, make sure life is better for Tommy than it was for you and Diego."

Jessica nodded, not trusting herself to say anything else. Maria was being extremely generous with her, and she didn't want to risk bursting into tears, although that's exactly what she felt like doing.

For Jessica, the next few days were unexpectedly peaceful. Tommy was a joy, delighting both his newly discovered grandmother and his grandfather. The three of them were often together, off on some big adventure, even though they couldn't leave the ranch.

Diego kept his distance, but Jessica could feel a bond building between them. She had forgotten what it was like to have a good friend, someone she could go to anytime, with any worry, and just talk.

Some evenings, Diego was very tired when he came in and the two of them would spend long, quiet hours sitting on the balcony outside their rooms, doing nothing more exciting than listening to the crickets and watching the brilliant stars high above in the summer sky.

They talked about everything on those nights.

And always when they said good night, Diego's kisses were restrained. She wondered if this restraint and denial was killing him as much as it was her.

On the weekend, Maria volunteered to cook dinner, a favorite Mexican dish that both Jessica and her father loved. That evening was one of the happiest Jessica could remember, with everyone feeling companionable, enjoying the traditional recipe that had been in Maria's family for years.

"You wouldn't consider coming back to work for me, would you?" Frank glanced up from his plate with appreciation.

"Dad," Jessica scolded.

But Maria laughed. Frank's teasing didn't seem to bother her at all. Apparently, with her son's help, she was putting many of her past hurts behind her, as well, and she had become a proud, assertive woman who knew exactly what she wanted and what she didn't want—and that included taking no guff from Frank McLean.

"For the right price," Maria said, using the same bantering tone as Frank, "who knows?"

"Boy, I'd like that, Grandma," Tommy said. "I'd like it if we all lived here together—you and Grandpa and Diego and Mom and me. That would be cool."

Jessica glanced at Diego, but he gave away nothing of his feelings in his expression. Neither of them had ever asked Tommy to call Diego Dad, but she couldn't help wondering if it bothered Diego that Tommy still called him by his name.

After Rosie took Tommy up to bed, the four adults sat talking over coffee.

"What about Colby?" Frank asked.

"The hearing is Monday. By then we should know which way the wind blows. If he's denied bail, I think we can relax a bit. If not . . ."

"Are the Rangers planning on keeping you and your men here through the trial?"

Diego shrugged. "We'll probably cut down on the number of men. But, yeah, if we can get a quick trial, get your testimony on record, then it could be over in a few months."

"If his slick lawyers don't delay it," Frank said.

"I don't think that's going to happen. Not with Judge Ambrose sitting on the trial. He's one of the toughest judges in this part of the country, and when he says we go to trial, you'd better believe we go to trial, no matter who Colby has for a lawyer."

Frank took a deep breath, seeming a little more relaxed after Diego's explanation. "Good. All I want to do is get this behind us so we can get back to our lives."

"Amen to that," Diego said, lifting his cup of coffee.

His eyes met Jessica's and she looked away.

She couldn't bear to think of his leaving. Now that he'd come back into her life, despite the barriers between them, she wanted him to stay.

But for tonight, she didn't want to think about that. She just wanted to enjoy the weekend and the peace she'd found being with her family. That's what she considered Diego and his mother now—part of their family. No matter how it ended, for now that was a good feeling.

On Monday morning, Diego came to her room early to tell her he was driving to El Paso for the hearing.

"My men are stationed at the gates and at the video monitors. But in case one of them misses something, don't let anyone in unless you know them personally," he said. "And don't go outside the gates for any reason."

"Yes, sir, Ranger, sir," she said with a mock salute.

They were standing very close. Jessica reached out and straightened a button on Diego's shirt, then looked up into his face. She pushed her fingers inside his shirt, tugging at the material and pulling him closer.

They came together slowly, their lips meeting in a kiss that was long and deep and sweet.

"I hate to leave you," he whispered.

"And I hate for you to go." She stood on tiptoe and placed another kiss against his mouth.

With a soft groan, he pulled her into his arms, crushing her against him and kissing her hungrily.

When they pulled away this time, both of them were trembling.

"We'll be fine here until you get back," she said. "Don't worry."

"I'll be back as soon as I can."

"I'll be waiting," she whispered.

Diego left the ranch and drove toward El Paso. The road was as straight as an arrow and there was little traffic. That was good, because he couldn't concentrate on anything except Jessica and the way she had looked at him when he left.

For a long time he'd felt there was something missing from his life. He'd worked hard and played hard in an effort to find whatever it was. Women weren't hard to find, but none of them ever seemed to be the right one.

If he were honest, none of them ever stood up to a comparison with Jessica, his first love. Hell, his only love, if he would only let himself admit it.

But it wasn't only the loss of Jessica that caused a big void in his life. He hadn't known until recently exactly what it was he'd been looking for.

Now he did.

The sweet, unquestioning love he saw between Jessica and Tommy drew him in like unsuspecting prey into a web. He gravitated toward it, felt its warmth. And he wanted it, needed it as a thirsty man needs water.

He wanted a family, and he wanted to belong to that family truly and completely. He wanted them to belong to him the same way. Someone he could count on and cherish. Defend. Someone to run to when his day and his work left him feeling troubled and uncertain about the world he lived in.

Then, like a prayer answered, it had dropped right into his lap.

Tommy had given him unconditional love even before he learned Diego was his father.

And today, in Jessica's eyes, he thought he saw the same thing.

She was his for the taking, and this time he was

beginning to believe she wanted him for who he was, in spite of who he was.

He had to put his defensiveness and resentments behind him if he expected that to happen. He had to let go of the past and the feeling he had never been good enough for Jessica. He had to find the strength and the courage to reach out and grab the golden ring.

And as for Jessica, he wanted to banish the sadness that lingered behind her eyes. He wanted it gone forever. He wanted to see her smile, hear her laughter ringing through the house.

And he wanted to be the one responsible for that.

EIGHTEEN

After Diego left, Jessica had a hard time concentrating on anything except his kiss and the way he had held her.

She thought there had been a promise in his eyes, an anticipation, but she dared not let herself hope too much. Not yet.

She would find herself sitting at her desk, gazing off into space, lost in the remembrance of his voice. She went over every look, every word he'd said.

Then, with a sigh and a self-deprecating grin, she'd force herself back to work.

Tommy was in and out of her office all day and finally ended up playing on the patio outside. They had a pleasant lunch with Maria.

"Oh, my," Maria said, shaking her head over the delicious avocado and chicken salad. "I think after this I'm going to have to take a nap."

"Well, why not? Pamper yourself a little. I'm sure Tommy has worn you out these past few days."

"Oh, not at all." Maria smiled and reached out to touch Tommy's hair. "He's a joy."

"Yes," Jessica said with a knowing smile, "but sometimes even joy can be wearing. Take a nap. Do whatever you feel like doing."

"Better be careful," Maria said. "I'm feeling completely spoiled."

"Good, you deserve it. Tommy, we're going to let your grandmother rest now. You can play in my office the rest of the day, OK?"

"Can I bring my soldiers and play on the patio?"

"May I," Jessica corrected.

"May I?" he asked, grinning.

"You may."

Jessica hadn't been back in her office long when the intercom on her desk buzzed.

She pushed the red button.

"Yes?"

"Miss McLean, this is Hank at the front gate. We have a gentleman here who says he wants to see you."

Jessica frowned and her heart pounded a bit faster than usual. She remembered Diego's warning about letting anyone in she didn't know, but she hadn't expected that to be a problem she'd have to handle.

"Who is it, Hank?"

"Says his name is Red Ogle. Says he worked for you the past few years and you told him to come back for a summer job whenever he got finished with his job in New Mexico."

Jessica breathed a sigh of relief and smiled. "Of

course. Red's worked here several times. I'll be happy to see him, Hank. Send him on in."

Jessica went back to work, knowing one of the maids would let Red in. She glanced out through the open patio doors to where Tommy was playing.

In a few minutes she heard a knock at her door and stood up from behind her desk. "Come in."

Red Ogle walked into the room. He was a tall, lanky man, probably no more than forty, but he looked older. His dark skin was weathered from years in the sun and the jeans he wore were faded almost white.

Jessica reached out and the man took off his grimy cowboy hat and reached across the desk to shake her hand.

"Hello, Red. It's good to see you again. How was New Mexico?"

"Hotter'n Hades," he said, his Texas twang very pronounced. "They need rain bad. Had a lot of crop failures, so jobs were hard to come by. Thought I'd drop by here on my way up north, see if you all need any ranch hands. Temporary will be fine."

"We can always use experienced ranch hands." Jessica nodded. "And you've always done good work. You can start today. You know where the bunkhouse is."

She noticed him looking over her shoulder to the patio.

"Your boy's grown." He grinned.

"He sure has."

He nodded toward the door. "What's with all the

new gates and guards? I don't recall as McLean ranch had any of that last year."

"No, you're right—that is something new. We've had a few problems with break-ins. Dad thought we needed a little extra security." Even though she knew Red, she felt a little funny telling him more than that.

"Some of them boys got a look about 'em."

"What do you mean?" she asked.

"You know how lawmen have that certain look, that clean-cut look . . . short hair, sunglasses."

Jessica's laugh was short and forced.

"Dad might have found some retired deputies, for all I know." She looked down at her desk, pushing a few papers about.

"Well, none of my business," he said, his voice soft and apologetic. "Didn't mean to be nosy."

"It's fine, Red. Just let me know if you need anything."

"Will do. Thanks mighty kindly, Miss McLean."

She watched him walk from the room, wondering at the odd tingle that raced up her spine.

What was it about him that set her teeth on edge? She wasn't sure. Maybe it wasn't Red at all. Maybe all the worry and tension of the last few weeks was getting to her.

In any case, she'd be glad when Diego got back from El Paso.

She glanced again at the patio, but Tommy was nowhere in sight. Jessica ran to the door.

"Tommy?" she asked, her voice breathless.

"I'm over here, Mom." He was playing in the

dirt a few feet off the patio, toward the front of the house.

She breathed a heavy sigh and walked back to her desk.

"I don't know what on earth is wrong with me today," she muttered to herself. "Jumpy as a jack-rabbit."

No more than fifteen minutes later, Maria stuck her head around the door.

"Have you seen my grandson?" She smiled warmly at Jessica. "After a nap, I have my second wind."

"Are you sure?" Jessica laughed. She leaned back in her chair and stretched her arms over her head, feeling the tension in her shoulders and neck.

"Of course I'm sure. I thought I'd take him off your hands for a little while, if you don't mind. Go to the kitchen, get some cookies and milk and take them outside with us, just wander around in the courtyard." Maria stepped into the room.

"I think I'll join you. I've been at this long enough today. I could use a break."

"Great."

They walked to the patio doors. Jessica glanced out in the yard where she'd seen Tommy just a few minutes earlier.

He wasn't there.

"Tommy?" She scanned the entire area. "Tommy!" she screamed.

She felt Maria's hand on her arm. "Jessica, what's wrong?"

"He was here . . . just a moment ago. And then Red came and—oh, God . . . Red!"

"Jessica—sweetheart, listen to me." Maria took Jessica's shoulders and turned the younger woman to face her. "You're not making any sense."

Jessica was trembling, and the thought of standing there calmly and explaining everything to Maria made her want to scream. She managed to tell her about Red and about the feeling of dread she'd had when he left.

"And now Tommy's disappeared. I have to find him. I can't stand here any longer and—"

"Calm down. Tommy's probably here. He could have wandered around to the kitchen. He could be anywhere."

"No, this isn't like him. He would never go somewhere without telling me."

Maria smiled indulgently. "We'll find him."

"Find who?"

Jessica turned with a start and saw Diego standing just inside her office.

The sight of him, the relief she felt, made her knees grow weak and for a moment, she felt them buckle beneath her.

"Diego. Oh, God, Diego." She went toward him, hands outstretched.

Then she was in his arms, those strong arms that could always comfort, always reassure her the world was all right. For a moment she could almost believe it was.

Her words came out in a jumble, first explaining

about Tommy's being on the patio, then about Red.

"I told him he had a job and he went to put his things in the bunkhouse. And now Tommy's gone."

Diego's eyes narrowed and he reached out, grabbing her shoulders and staring into her eyes.

"What have you done?" he asked. "I can't believe this. After I explained to you, after I warned you not to let anyone in here, you did it anyway?" His fury was alive, like something that might reach out and grab Jessica at any moment.

She flinched from his anger, her mouth working soundlessly as she tried to understand his rage.

"You said not to let anyone in I didn't know."

He wasn't listening. He had his hands on his hips and looked as if he were about to bolt.

She reached out, taking his shirt as if she would not let him go.

"Listen to me! Is this the way its always going to be between us, you always second guessing me? I knew this man, Diego. I had no reason to suspect him of anything. He's worked here several years."

His eyes changed and he frowned. He'd heard her this time, but she doubted it would satisfy him.

"Are you ever going to trust me again?" she asked, her voice quiet. She was shaking now almost uncontrollably, but as she stared into Diego's eyes, she felt herself pulling away from him mentally.

He stepped around her, not answering, and went to the phone on the desk.

"What's this man's name? Give me a description.

In the meantime, Mother, you and Jessica get help. Call Hank at the front post. Have the house and grounds searched."

Through lips grown stiff with fear, Jessica managed to do as he asked. Within seconds Diego was on the phone with headquarters in Austin, having Red's name run through their computers.

Maria had been standing back silently, but now, when Jessica turned to her, she opened her arms and Jessica mutely stepped into the woman's embrace.

"It will be all right, darling," she said. "We'll find him. You get Hank on the intercom and I'll go find your father. Together we'll search the house."

Jessica swallowed hard and nodded. She took a deep breath, telling herself Maria was right. She had to believe that.

"Meet us back here in fifteen minutes." Jessica moved toward the intercom.

"Hank, have you seen Tommy? Did he come all the way out to the gates?" She explained quickly about Red Ogle.

"Do you know where he went? Is his car at the bunkhouse?"

"Bunkhouse?" Hank asked. "He didn't go to the bunkhouse when he left the house. He hightailed it out of here in that old beat-up car of his soon as he got through the gate. Oh, my God," Hank muttered beneath his breath.

"What was he driving? Never mind. Come to my

office. You can give Diego the descriptions. It will
save time."

Jessica sank into her chair, her head in her
hands. She heard Diego hang up the phone,
heard his heavy sigh, and looked up at him.

His eyes were grief stricken, a look she'd never
seen there before. She stood up, hardly aware of
what she was doing.

"He has a record," Diego said quietly. "And
Ogle is just one of his aliases. Last time he was
arrested, he was working for Lamar Colby. The
hearing was postponed today. Now I know why.
Colby had one last trick up his sleeve."

His words rang like a death knell in the room.

Jessica could hardly speak or respond. But she
could no longer stand.

She sat in the chair at her desk, holding her
hands over her mouth.

"No, no, no. He has Tommy." Her tears came
in a flood, washing down her face as she looked
up at Diego. "He has our little boy, Diego. He's
so little. My God, he must be so scared. And it's
my fault, my—"

"Sweetheart, don't . . ."

Diego took one step forward, pulling her up out
of the chair and into his arms. Her arms were
limp as he held her, rocking her back and forth
and making soft, quieting noises in her ear.

"It isn't your fault. It isn't anyone's fault. There
was no way you could know. You knew this man.
There was no reason not to trust him. You haven't
done anything wrong." He pulled back, reaching

out and brushing her hair out of her face and
lifting her chin with his fingers. "You hear me?"
he asked. "I'm so sorry for accusing you. You
don't deserve that. You're the best mother in the
world and you've done nothing wrong."

With a quiet sob, she fell against him, crying
against his shoulder as he held her, letting all her
fears and guilt out.

"Forgive me," he whispered.

She couldn't speak. She could only nod against
his shirt.

"We're going to find him," he said, his voice
fierce. "I promise you that, Jess. Together, you and
I. We're going to find our boy."

NINETEEN

Within thirty minutes, they knew without a doubt Tommy was not in the house or on the grounds.

Then the phone call came. Frank McLean answered, putting the phone on speaker. The message was short and to the point.

"We got the kid, McLean. He won't get hurt if you do exactly as I say. All you have to do is forget about testifying against Colby and the boy will be returned, safe and sound. You got that?"

"Yes." Frank's voice cracked. "I understand."

"You get in touch with the D.A. right now. Tell them you've changed your mind. Tell them you're afraid. Tell 'em you don't know anything after all. We don't care what you say. We'll get the word. And don't worry, we'll see you never spend a day in jail." The man laughed deviously. "Soon as Colby is set free, we'll let the boy go. And, McLean . . . if you ever want to see the kid again, you won't tell anyone about this. No cops, no feds."

"All right," Frank said. "Anything you want. But you have to tell me where—"

"I don't have to tell you anything, man. We'll be in touch."

Frank looked at Diego, waiting for instructions, but before anyone could respond, the caller hung up.

Jessica gasped aloud, reaching forward as if she might bring the voice back. For those few brief moments when the kidnapper had been on the speaker phone, Jessica had felt a physical connection with Tommy. But now it was gone, broken, and she felt as helpless as she'd ever felt in her life. She picked up one of the little green plastic soldiers she'd brought in from the patio, the toys Tommy had been playing with.

She turned to Diego and saw the same deep fear, the same anguish in his eyes. The connection between them at that moment was a living, breathing bond.

Without thinking, she went to him and put her arms around him, not caring that Maria and her father were in the room watching. She wanted his comfort and she knew he needed to feel her arms around him as much as she needed to feel his.

"We have one advantage that I can see," Diego said, still holding Jessica tightly in his arms. "Evidently they don't know the Rangers are here."

"Red asked about the security at the gates and I told him we'd had some break-ins. Thank goodness your men are in plainclothes."

"You did the right thing." He touched her face gently. "Let's just hope he bought it."

Just then the intercom on the desk clicked on and Diego walked quickly to lean over it, listening.

"Yeah, Hank. You got something?"

"They just found Ogle's old car abandoned on the road about five miles from here. No one in it."

Diego's men were all so stoic, so professional and cool, that Jessica was surprised to hear the quiet hint of concern and sympathy in Hank's voice. It was almost as if Diego's Rangers were a part of Tommy's family now.

Diego nodded and took a deep breath, looking into Jessica's eyes as if searching for answers. She thought it was the first time she'd ever seen him at such a loss, as if he hardly knew which way to turn. It was unlike him to show his vulnerability, and it made her want to cry, made her want to throw herself in his arms and soothe away his fears, kiss away his anguish.

He leaned over and pushed the intercom button again.

"Anything else, Hank?"

"Looks like two horses heading east through brush country, maybe toward the Sierra Diablos."

"It's going to be too late for helicopters in a few hours."

"Yep," Hank said. "He probably figured on that, too. Once they're in the mountains, it's going to be hard for anyone to spot them from the air.

And, Diego"—Hank hesitated—"on the ground where the horses were, they found something."

"What?" Diego's voice cracked only the slightest bit.

"A toy soldier. Green. You know, the kind kids play with."

Diego looked at the toy Jessica still held and his mouth thinned into a tight line.

"That son of a—" he muttered. "If he hurts Tommy, I swear I'll—"

"Boss, you heard what I said about the toy soldier?"

"Yeah, I heard you. He has Tommy all right, Hank. He was playing with those same soldiers before he disappeared from the house."

"Need me to do anything?"

"Just stand by. I'll let you know." Diego turned to Jessica. "I'm going after him. If we wait till morning, he's going to be so far ahead of us we'll never find him. I have a hunch he's making his way up to the mountain to be picked up, either by plane or helicopter."

"You can't go by yourself." Worry showed in her green eyes.

"If they get a hint that an army of Rangers is after him, we'll lose all chance of getting Tommy back." He looked deep into her eyes. "I have to do this, Jess. It's the only way we have a chance. You'll have to trust me enough to bring our son back."

"I'm going with you, and it has nothing to do with whether I trust you or not."

"Oh, no." He shook his head and moved away from her as if he knew she could change his mind with one touch or one look. "You're not going, Jess, and that's final. I'm not going to put your life in jeopardy along with Tommy's."

"I'm going, too." Her eyes sparkled defiantly. "I can shoot as well as you, and I can ride better, in case you've forgotten."

"Jess, don't you understand? It isn't that you aren't capable. Hell, I know you can handle yourself as well as, if not better than, most men. And I don't want to leave you behind, but what would I do—what would Tommy do if I let you go and something happened to you? I couldn't live with myself if that happened."

"And I couldn't live if I let you go alone and something happened to you," she said, her voice strong and firm.

Diego frowned as if someone had just struck him. He rubbed his hand down his face and stared deeply into her eyes.

For a moment it was as if they were alone in the room.

"Jessie, damn it . . ."

Frank McLean coughed. When Jessica turned to him, she saw Maria standing there, her eyes filled with tears as she watched her son and Jessica.

"You may as well say yes, son," Frank said. "You know how stubborn she is when she sets her mind on something. Besides, she's right. My guess is you could use another rifle out there."

Diego let the air out of his lungs and his hands

moved restlessly at his side. He walked to the patio door, gazing out toward the mountains. For those few minutes, the room behind him went completely silent.

"All right." He turned. "Get dressed and get your gear. I'm leaving in twenty minutes. If you aren't ready, I'm going without you."

Jessica knew he meant exactly what he said. She didn't say another word, and there was no joy or triumph on her face. She simply turned and hurried from the room, touching her father's arm as she passed.

Twenty minutes later, they were telling Maria and Frank good-bye.

"I know you're going to find him, son." With tears in her eyes, Maria reached up and hugged her tall, handsome son. "I'm so proud of you," she said. "And I love you."

"I love you, too, Mom. Don't worry."

"We'll be waiting for you to bring Tommy home." Frank reached out to shake Diego's hand.

Jessica had seen her father cry only once, but today she saw the glitter in his eyes that had been there when her mother died.

"I haven't said it in so many words," he said, "but I'm proud of you, too, and I couldn't ask for a better man to be the father of my grandson. I trust you, Diego. If anyone can find him, I know you can."

Jessica put her arms around her father, felt his awkward, reassuring pat on her back.

BENEATH A TEXAS MOON   227

"Thank you, Daddy," she whispered. "I love you."

"And I love you, too, girl." With a loud sniff, Frank pulled away, standing stiff and erect as he turned to Diego.

"You take care of my little girl, now," he said, with an attempt at his old gruffness.

"I'll do my best, Mr. McLean."

Jessica could see Diego's impatience. He wanted to go, and so did she. But both of them needed this good-bye with their parents in case something went wrong.

That frightened her more than she could say, and she quickly pushed the thought from her mind.

"I can't ask for more than that," Frank said. "Now better get on. It's getting late."

With one last, hurried wave, Diego and Jessica left the room. Outside, their horses were saddled and ready, their saddlebags stuffed with supplies and bedrolls strung behind the saddles. On each horse was a long leather case holding a rifle. Diego checked to make sure they had extra cartridges.

"You have the cell phone?" he asked.

"Yes, and extra batteries."

They mounted up, not speaking again as they left the house. Jessica didn't look back. She couldn't let saying good-bye to Maria and her father distract her. She had only one purpose in mind now, and that was finding Tommy. She would

have to leave behind her sadness about leaving
home. Being with Diego made that possible.

When she was with him, she *was* home.

They stopped for a moment at the front gate
and got a map and a quick briefing from Hank
about where the car had been found.

"Their tracks lead due east," he said. "He knows
the area. They'll have to stay that course in order
to cross the creek at its shallowest point. If you
cut across right here"—Hank tapped the map—
"you should intersect with their trail in about
twenty minutes—thirty tops."

Diego nodded, took the map and stuffed it into
his saddlebag. Then, with a questioning look at
Jessica, and her answering nod, they rode out.

The men stationed at the gate waved, and several murmured quiet wishes of good luck.

They rode briskly, taking the shorter route they
hoped would intersect with Ogle's trail. Jessica's
chest tightened with apprehension. What if they
missed the trail and had to backtrack, losing precious time? They had to make it to the foothills
before nightfall if they were to have a chance at
catching up with them at all.

Later, when Diego pulled up in front of her, she
held her breath wondering if something was
wrong. When he pointed to tracks on the ground,
she breathed a quiet little sigh of relief.

"This is it." He turned to look at her.

She smiled at the look of relief deep in his eyes,
for she knew, no matter how bravely he hid it, he

had the same doubts, the same apprehensions she did.

She moved her horse closer to his so she could see the tracks.

"They look fresh. It has to be them." There was a question in her eyes.

He drew himself up in the saddle and turned around to look over his shoulder, lifting his arm as if aiming down it.

"It's almost a straight line from here to where they found the car."

"You're right," she said.

He looked at her for one long moment, then reached across, putting his arm around her and pulling her to him.

"I guess I usually just trust my gut instinct in situations like this," he said, his face very close to hers.

"I know. But since Tommy's involved . . ." She nodded her understanding.

"We saved time by cutting across, but now I almost wish we'd gone to the car and started there. Then we'd have known for sure."

"You can't doubt yourself now, Diego. You've been doing this for a long time and you know what you're doing. You're an expert. I trust you, Diego. You have to trust yourself and do what you'd do if this were some ordinary little boy and not our son."

He was looking at her with such tenderness that it almost took her breath away. He kissed her, a kiss of sweet yearning and gratitude. And when they pulled away, his eyes were shining and warm.

"You have no idea what it means to me to hear you say that. Your trust means a lot."

"I *do* trust you. I trust you with my life, Diego. More than that, I trust you with the most precious thing I have in the world . . . our little boy."

"I guess this is the perfect time to clear up one thing between us, angel. I trust you, too. I was wrong to blame you for what your father did, and I was wrong to leave with no explanation. I should have known you'd never be a part of such a scheme."

"Oh, Diego . . ."

"And I say we make a pact, here and now," he whispered. "We're in this together, no matter what happens—no matter how it ends."

She couldn't speak for a moment, and she wondered if he had any idea how much it meant to her, hearing him say those words. She wanted his trust more than anything.

"It will end the way we want it to," she said, leaning forward for another kiss. "It has to."

TWENTY

It was growing dark, and they still had not made it to the foothills of the mountains. Finally Diego pulled his horse to a stop and reached out to grab the reins on Jessica's mount. "We'll have to camp here."

"But it's only a few miles to the tree line." Jessica pointed ahead.

"It's dark, baby. We have to stop. If we go on, we take a chance of losing the trail in the dark. The horses can't see as well, and we'd be taking a chance that one of them will stumble or step in a hole. We can't risk it, Jess."

She could see by the look on his face that he wanted to go on as much as she did.

"You're right." She swung her leg over the saddle and dismounted.

Her back and neck felt stiff, and it seemed as if every muscle in her body ached. She was used to riding, but not the way they'd ridden today.

She bent and stretched, groaning. "Yes, you're definitely right," she said, attempting a smile. "It was time to stop."

They were beginning to leave the arid brushland behind. In the last hour, they'd begun seeing a few clumps of trees here and there. They were near a little stream, and beneath the trees it seemed cooler. There was even a small patch of grass nearby for the horses.

Diego handed Jessica their bedrolls and another bag containing food. He unsaddled and tended the horses, then led them to the grassy spot beneath the trees and tied them.

By the time he finished, Jessica had a blanket spread and their sleeping bags arranged on top of it. She groaned slightly as she sank slowly onto the blanket and opened their bag of food.

"Tired?" Diego asked, standing above her.

"I hate to admit how tired I am," she said wearily. "I wish I could go on. I wish we could ride all night."

She gritted her teeth, thinking of Tommy and how he must be feeling. Was he scared? He was bound to be confused and missing her and Diego now. Somehow this time of day, just before dark, always seemed sad and lonesome when you were separated from the ones you loved.

He sat down across from her and took off his Stetson, placing it on the ground above his sleeping bag. He picked up a bottle of water and opened it, handing it to her before opening another for himself.

"He's fine, you know." He looked at her from beneath lowered brows.

"Oh, Diego," she whispered, suddenly near

tears. "He's so little. And he must be so afraid right now."

"You're his mother, so I'm sure you see different qualities in him than I do. But I'm telling you right now he might be little, but he's smart, Jessica."

There was pride in his voice, and the confidence with which he spoke buoyed Jessica's spirits.

"How many kids his age would think to leave those soldiers along the trail?" He reached across, cupping her chin in his hand and trying hard not to concentrate on her lush, trembling mouth.

"Not many," she admitted with a small, wistful smile. She sniffed and wiped at her eyes, determined not to cry.

"You've done a good job with him," he said. "He's smart and funny and mischievous, yet he knows how to behave and be respectful. You've done that, Jessica."

"Diego," she began, wanting to apologize again for exempting him from his son's life. "I didn't mean—"

His hand caressed her face. "Don't say it. That's all in the past now."

"Do you mean it?"

"I do." He shrugged his broad shoulders. Then, with a grin that reminded her of Tommy, he said, "Hell, I don't even know myself how I came to this conclusion. It just happened."

"I'm so happy to hear you say it," she whispered.

"I couldn't ask for a better son than the boy

you raised, Jessica. And I'm hoping by the time
he's ten or so, he won't even remember when I
wasn't in his life . . . when he didn't have a dad."

"Oh," she said through trembling lips. "I hope
for that, too. I do."

"OK." He moved away from her and reached
into the bag of food. "No more regrets. We're going to eat and drink, get a good night's sleep, and
tomorrow, Jess, I promise you, if it's the last thing
I do, we're going to have our boy back."

Jessica took a deep breath and began to eat. She
hadn't felt hungry. But now, she was beginning to
see it from another perspective—from Diego's view
as a Texas Ranger. He couldn't afford to let emotions stand in the way. She understood exactly
what his practical words meant, and she knew he
was right. If they expected to find Tommy, they
had to take care of themselves first. They couldn't
go to the point of exhaustion and then lose out
on the chance to rescue him when that time came.

But deep down inside, she didn't think she
would be able to sleep a wink tonight thinking
about how alone and scared her baby was.

They couldn't risk a campfire. When the sun
went down, Jessica thought she'd never seen a
night so dark. They lay side by side, but in sepa-
rate sleeping bags.

Diego reached out and found her hand, giving
her strength and warmth and making her feel not
so alone. He lay looking up at the stars and the
waning moon. He could feel the tension in Jessica's fingers. Hell, he could almost read her

thoughts, for he knew they were the same as his. It seemed impossible they could even consider sleeping while Tommy was out there somewhere, alone and frightened.

Diego moved his shoulders restlessly, wanting to shake off those feelings. He couldn't let them interfere in what he had to do.

But he couldn't stop thinking about Tommy any more than he could stop thinking about the woman who lay so quietly at his side.

When they'd gotten into their bedrolls, there had sprung up a new tension between them. Even though nothing had been said, he wondered if she needed to be held as much as he wanted to hold her.

Jessica had always seemed serene and calm. But these last few hours, he had seen her composure slowly disintegrating. It broke his heart. And yet instead of reaching out for him, she seemed to grow more distant.

A man knows when a woman wants to be held, needs to be kissed, yearns to be loved. Tonight, all he felt from Jessica was her need to be alone, to be lost in her thoughts of Tommy. He would give her the space she needed, no matter how much it killed him inside.

He had just drifted off to sleep when a sound woke him.

He lay very still for a moment, then realized the sound came from Jessica. She was trying hard to hide it, but he knew she was crying. Her hand was no longer in his, and she had turned over onto her side, facing away from him.

Her shoulders trembled in the dim moonlight.

"Jess?"

Jessica became very still, holding her breath when she heard Diego's voice. She wanted to be strong for him. What would he think of her if he knew what a coward she was inside, how scared she really was? The last thing she wanted was for him to think she no longer trusted him to find Tommy. But she couldn't help it. As soon as she'd closed her eyes, all she saw was Tommy's face, his big brown eyes, pleading and lost.

"Jessie," Diego said, his voice tender. He reached out, pulling her around to face him.

In the darkness his hand touched her face, coming away wet from the tears on her cheeks. His breath caught in his throat when she came to him clumsily, shaking, her sobs no longer hidden. She moved over beside him, her arms wrapping tightly around him as if he were her lifeline.

"Baby, what is it? Tell me."

"I just feel so lost," she sobbed. "As if the world has stopped and everything is dead. I . . . I keep seeing his face, Diego. I can't help it. I just can't stop seeing his little face." Her words sent her into another paroxysm of sobs.

Diego held her tighter, smoothing her hair away from her hot face, whispering soft words to comfort her.

"I'm sorry. I don't mean to fall apart on you. But I'm scared, Diego. I'm just so afraid."

"Cry all you want, angel. Get it all out. Hell, I feel like crying myself."

It was strange how quickly, being in his arms, hearing his voice, she began to feel better.

She even managed a little laugh at his words.

He rocked her in his arms, like a child. At the moment, all he wanted was to comfort her, to hold her.

Jessica sighed and snuggled her head against his chest. Her hair brushed his face and her soft breasts pressed against him, sending a jolt of desire through him. He lay very still, willing it to go away, not wanting anything to spoil this moment.

Jessica could feel his heart beating against her breasts, its steady, rhythmic sound keeping time with her own racing pulse. Her hand moved up to touch his neck, then his face.

She let her fingers wander over his skin, gently touching the scar on his shoulder before moving her head to place a soft kiss there. Diego's strong body shuddered as her hands moved up to his face. She felt the stubble of beard beneath his skin, then the soft warmth of his mouth.

She felt his swift intake of air, felt the tension in his hard body.

"Jess," he growled, his voice a quiet warning.

"Shhh, don't say anything. Just let me . . ." She wrapped her arms around him, moving up and kissing him beneath the curve of his jaw, letting her lips feel the warm, living pulse of his heart.

With a groan, he lifted her up and on top of

him. She whispered his name, searching in the darkness and finding his mouth.

Their kiss was hungry, filled with all the desire they had repressed over the past few days. Something else was there as well—a need for comfort so strong neither of them could deny it.

Diego pulled off his shirt and pushed hers away from her body. Her skin was hot, on fire against his.

He kissed her until she gasped for breath, then came back for more. Neither of them seemed able to get enough, to touch enough.

Her hands trembled at the waistband of his jeans. With a quiet groan, he helped her, tearing them away as she quickly slid out of her own.

He rolled her over onto her back, taking her mouth again, hearing her wild, almost incoherent words of need as he took her body with his own.

Neither of them held back anything. This was not the moment for waiting, for denying anything. Their need was much too great. On the edge of wild desperation, they moved together, her hands clinging to him, his mouth urging her to give herself up completely.

Jessica quickly felt the waves envelop her, felt the powerful movements of his body and her own answering ones as she cried out his name again and again in the darkness.

"Sweet . . . oh, my sweet Jessie," he groaned, letting himself go over the edge into an overwhelming surge of pleasure.

Later they lay wrapped in each other's arms as the night wind caressed their bodies, cooling them.

Jessica had never felt so completely sedated in her life. She lay against his chest, letting her fingers caress his smooth skin.

"Oh, Diego," she whispered, brushing her lips against his skin. "I love you. I've loved you all my life, but never more than now."

He held her closer, tighter against him and brushed his lips against her hair, not trusting himself to say anything. He reached out and pulled the other sleeping bag over their naked bodies, murmuring soft words to her, holding her and promising he would never let her go.

They slept then, their exhaustion forcing them to give in to the warmth of their bodies entwined and to the blissful satisfaction of their heated lovemaking.

When Jessica awoke the next morning, she was alone. It was just becoming light, but the sun had not yet topped the hills. The scent of bacon and coffee hung in the air, making her stomach growl hungrily. She smiled and turned over, seeing Diego kneeling near a small fire.

For a moment she felt a thrill of happiness, seeing his strong, beautiful body and remembering the night. Only when she realized where she was and why did she frown and think of Tommy.

She threw the covers back and quickly pulled on her jeans.

"Hey." Diego turned to smile at her.

"Morning," she said, almost shyly.

"I thought a small fire wouldn't be noticed in the daylight, but we'll probably have to eat on the road."

"That's fine." She glanced toward the hills. "Do you think we can catch them today?"

"We'll catch them." He looked toward the mountains, too. "Having a little boy along is bound to slow him down."

He came to her, squatting down near the blanket on which they'd slept and handing her a cup of steaming coffee. When she took the cup, their hands touched and lingered.

"How are you?" His eyes moved slowly, sweetly over her.

"I would say wonderful," she said, unable to hide the love she felt, "if not for the circumstances."

He leaned over and kissed her, then came to his feet and began to gather up their things.

"You rest," he said when she started to get up. "Drink your coffee, walk down to the stream and wash your face. I'll have everything packed up when you get back."

For one moment as she walked to the stream, Jessica allowed herself to imagine this was a normal day, that they could linger here as long as they wished, make love again, sleep in the shade of the trees until noon, wake in each other's arms, and make love again.

Then she tucked those thoughts away, telling herself that one day her dream might actually come true.

TWENTY-ONE

By the time the sun rose over the mountains, they were in the foothills, their horses slowly, arduously picking their way through the trees and over the rocks.

Ogle's trail converged with another, more well-worn trail up the mountains.

"Do you know this trail, Jess?" he asked, looking back at her over his shoulder.

"No, but I'm pretty sure we're no longer on private property."

Diego nodded and reached for the cell phone, calling Hank back at the ranch.

"We've come upon a well-used trail up the northwestern slope of the mountain, Hank. Ask Mr. McLean if he's familiar with it."

"He says it leads to an old abandoned line shack. Government property now, but sometimes the ranchers still use it when they're looking for stray cattle that wander into the mountains during hot weather. How you doin'?" Hank added. "See anything?"

"I have a feeling Ogle might be holed up at this

shack, maybe waiting for a ride. Has McLean received any other calls?"

"No, none. Want me to send the helicopter for backup?"

"Negative," Diego said firmly. "I don't want to spook him. If Ogle's the only one here, I can handle it."

"Let's hope he is the only one there," Hank said. "You can make it short and sweet."

Diego put the phone away, his glance meeting Jessica's as he told her what Hank had said.

"I remember hearing talk about the old line shack. It shouldn't be too much farther."

"Are you hungry?" he asked.

"Starving. But I can go on if—"

"Five minutes. We'll stretch our legs, give the horses a breather, and grab something out of the saddlebag. Five minutes won't make that much difference."

The five minutes worked wonders for Jessica. They came off their horses and immediately into each other's arms, as if it was something they were used to, something they'd been doing all their lives. They held each other, kissed, and gave each other reassurance.

"This is all I need," Diego said. "Just five minutes with you."

"Me, too." Her cheeks were flushed from the heat, her eyes sparkled from his kisses.

After the break, they pushed forward with added urgency.

By midmorning, the land began to level, and

they knew they were very close to the line shack. Diego held his hand back toward her, urging Jessica to go slowly. As soon as he caught the first glimpse of the gray, weathered building, he stepped off his horse and tied the reins to a tree. Jessica did the same, pulling her rifle from its scabbard and reaching into the bag for extra cartridges.

She stepped behind Diego and handed him a box of shells. He motioned her to the left, while he went to the right.

Her heart was pounding so loudly that it made a constant roar in her ears. She felt breathless, light-headed. For a moment, she feared she might actually faint.

"We have to find Tommy," she muttered through clenched teeth. "I can do this. I *have* to do this." She glanced toward Diego for support and saw him nod, motioning her forward.

They came up behind the cabin. There were no windows in the back of the building, and a thin wisp of smoke trailed from the chimney. The aroma of bacon lingered in the air.

Diego motioned toward a small lean-to in the woods beside the cabin where two horses were tied. Past the shack, an open space showed recent efforts at clearing. It looked as if Diego was right about Ogle waiting here to be picked up. Colby probably had a helicopter of his own waiting nearby.

Their time was limited. When Jessica saw Diego crouch low and move toward the house, she held her breath. He motioned her to stay back, and she moved her rifle up, cocking it and clicking a cartridge up into the chamber. She was shaking so badly she had to steady the rifle against a tree.

Once he reached the side of the cabin, Diego picked up a rock and threw it hard toward the lean-to and the horses. One of the horses jumped and whinnied, causing the other to buck and pull at its tether.

They waited long moments, and then Diego threw a second rock, causing more commotion in the lean-to.

Diego heard the front door open slowly. With his eyes steady on the front corner of the shack, he reached behind him and motioned Jessica forward.

She ran as fast as she could, coming up behind him and crouching down on one knee, lifting her rifle and waiting.

They could hear footsteps on the front porch. Then the sound stopped.

"Come on," Diego whispered. "Come on."

Red Ogle stepped off the porch, a pistol in one hand. He moved out into the yard, looking hard toward the lean-to. Diego flattened himself against the building and Jessica kept perfectly still.

Diego let the man walk several yards, far enough to make sure Tommy wasn't with him. Then he stood up, aiming his rifle slowly and deliberately.

"Drop the gun, Ogle," he shouted.

The man whirled around, pistol coming up. He

fired wildly, the bullet whizzing past them and off into the woods.

Simultaneously Diego fired, his shot hitting the man in the arm, spinning the pistol out of his hand and across the ground. Ogle turned and began to run, holding his arm as he went.

Diego made a step as if he might follow. Then he turned to Jessica, reaching down his hand to her.

"You OK?"

"Yes," she said, breathless. "Aren't you going after him?"

"Not till we find Tommy. He won't get far on foot."

They were cautious going around the front of the shack, still not sure if Ogle had met someone here or not.

The front door was closed and there was no sound at all from inside.

Jessica had never felt such fear before in her life. What if Tommy wasn't here? Dear God, she couldn't even let herself think about the possibility.

Diego motioned her to one side of the door while he stood on the other. Quickly he leaned back and kicked the door open with his foot.

The door swung back, slamming hard against the inside wall of the cabin. It was dim and shadowy inside.

Diego stepped to the door, his gaze moving swiftly from one side of the small room to the other and making sure no one else was there.

It seemed empty. For a moment, Jessica's heart dropped.

"Tommy?" Diego called.

On a small bunkbed in the corner, what looked like a pile of blankets began to move. Suddenly, Tommy sat up, rubbing his eyes and looking toward the doorway.

"Daddy!" he shouted, leaping down from the bed and racing across the room toward them. "Mommy!"

Diego and Jessica both fell to their knees, their arms open to receive their small son as he tumbled into them, wrapping his chubby arms around their necks.

"He called you Daddy," Jessica whispered to Diego. She could see the pride in his eyes and the love.

"You all right, son?" Diego asked. "Were you scared?"

"I knew you'd come and get me. That man said he was taking me to you, but I knew he wasn't." For the first time, Tommy's eyes darkened and his small chin trembled. "I left some soldiers for you to find," Tommy said, his voice rising bravely. "Just the way you told me. Did you find 'em, Daddy?"

"Yeah, son," Diego said, his voice cracking. "I found them. You're my good, brave boy. Daddy's proud of you."

Jessica was crying. When she looked into Diego's eyes, she saw tears there, and she reached across to kiss him.

"It's all right," she whispered. "You did it."

"*We* did it," he said, still holding on to her and Tommy. "I couldn't have done it without you, Jess. Let's go outside. Tommy, are you hungry?"

"Nope," Tommy said. "The man fed me. It wasn't good as home, but I wasn't hungry. Can we go home now, Daddy?"

Now that the word daddy had finally been spoken, Tommy couldn't seem to get enough of saying it. Jessica and Diego just grinned at each other.

"You bet, kid. You and your mom are going to rest while I ride down the mountain a little way, see if I can find the man who took you. Then we're going home."

Jessica took Tommy out onto the porch and leaned back against one of the posts. When she put her hand down onto the wood flooring, she felt a sharp sting and looked down to see a small scorpion skittering away from her.

"Oh, God." She jumped to her feet. "Here, Tommy, get away. There's a scorpion." She held her hand up and saw a small red circle beginning to form on the fleshy part of her palm.

Diego quickly stepped on the scorpion and reached across to take Jessica's hand.

"Let me see. Did it get you?"

"Let me see, too, Mommy."

"I'm OK. There's some sting kill in the saddle-bag."

"I'll get it." Diego hurried around the side of the cabin.

By the time he returned, the spot on her hand had turned into an ugly red welt that throbbed with every beat of her pulse. She held on to her wrist tightly, gritting her teeth.

"We have to get you out of here." He looked into her pain-filled eyes.

"I'm all right," she said. "What about the kidnapper? If you wait much longer, he might be gone for good."

He frowned at her, breaking an ampule of antiseptic and squeezing it onto her wound.

"Let him go," he said calmly.

"But . . ."

"I'm not leaving you," he said, his look incredulous. "Do you think I'd leave you up here alone with a scorpion sting to tend to?"

"I can take care of her, Daddy." Tommy puffed out his chest.

Diego grinned and ruffled Tommy's hair. "I know you can, sport. But I want to take care of her, too. OK?"

"OK," Tommy said, matter-of-factly. "We can both take care of her."

"Wow, I feel really lucky." But even as she tried to sound carefree, Jessica could feel her stomach churning with nausea. A fine sheen of perspiration broke across her forehead.

She stood up quickly and ran around the side of the house, where she was violently sick. When she straightened, Diego was beside her, his arm around her, holding her tightly.

"Has this ever happened before?" he asked, his voice filled with worry. "You're not allergic, are you?"

"I . . . I don't know," she said weakly as another spasm hit her. "I've never been stung by one before."

"God, where's the phone? I'm going to get that helicopter up here right now. Tommy," he shouted, "bring that canteen of water here for your mom and the first aid kit. There should be an antihistamine in it," he told Jessica.

Tommy hurried over, struggling a bit with the heavy pack and canteen, the look on his little face one of pride rather than concern. He wanted to help, and it was obvious he had no idea how ill Jessica was.

As they waited for the helicopter, Jessica thought she'd never felt sicker in her life. The only reassurance she could find was looking at Diego and Tommy as she told herself everything was going to be all right. It had to be. God wouldn't let her lose heaven now that she'd finally found it.

Jessica sat on the front porch, her back against the building, while Diego held her, brushing her hair back or washing her face with a cool cloth. Even as he kept an eye on Tommy playing in the yard, he murmured soft words into Jessica's ear.

"They'll be here soon, baby," he said. "How's your breathing? Does your throat feel OK?"

"Yes," she said weakly, reaching out to pull at his shirt. "Diego, I'm so sick."

"I know, baby. I know."

"I think I'm going to die."

"You're not going to die," he said, his voice fierce. "Don't even say such a thing. The helicopter will be here soon. I've already told them about the scorpion; they'll have epinephrine with them in case you need it."

"But if I should . . ." she began.

"You won't, damn it," he said.

"If anything happens to me, promise me you'll take Tommy. Dad is good. He loves Tommy, but I want him to be with you, Diego. Please, just promise me."

"God." He bent his head against hers and she heard and felt the quiet sobs that racked his chest. "Don't do this, Jessie."

"Will you, my darling?"

He lifted his head, looking deep into her eyes, tears streaming down his face.

"You don't even have to ask. Of course I will." He swallowed hard, clenching his teeth and willing himself to be strong.

In his heart, he knew she had just answered the question that always plagued him—whether or not he was good enough for the McLeans, whether he was worthy of being Tommy's father. Now that she had answered it, he found it didn't matter at all.

"I love you, Jessica," he said, suddenly afraid he would never have another chance to tell her.

Slowly she closed her eyes. She was smiling.

"Jessica?" he said, panic rising in him.

"I'm here," she whispered weakly. "I'm still here. I love you, too."

"You hang on, do you hear me? You're not going to leave me now, Jessica McLean. You got that?"

"Yes, sir, Ranger, sir," she murmured.

Less than an hour later, the helicopter landed in the clearing beyond the cabin, but for Diego it seemed like forever.

They gave Jessica a shot right away. By the time Diego had Tommy buckled into his seat and came back to her, Jessica was sleeping.

"She'll be fine," the pilot said. "Scorpions aren't deadly, but they can make you sick as hell sometimes. My guess is the worst of it is over by now. She'll probably sleep for hours, then she'll be fine."

The pilot had been right. After they got back to the ranch, Diego carried Jessica to her bed and she slept the rest of the day and on through the night. But despite Maria's and Rosie's offers to sit with her, Diego would not leave her side.

In the morning, just as the sun came up, she opened her eyes and saw Diego slumped in the chair beside her bed. She reached out and touched him, her heart leaping when he came awake and she saw the love and relief deep in his eyes.

"Jess," he whispered, moving toward her and taking her hands in his. "How are you feeling?" He looked at her bandaged hand and saw that the redness and swelling around it were almost gone.

"Am I home?" she asked, looking around the room.

"Yes, you're home," he said. "In your own bed. I guess you don't remember much about the helicopter ride off the mountain."

"The mountain." She pushed herself up in the bed. "Oh, God. Tommy . . ."

"Tommy's fine," he said, his hands gently urging her back down. "He's with Mom and he's fine. Colby's little escapade has insured him a place in prison for a long, long time. They caught Ogle, and he's willing to testify against Colby. Your father has gone today to give a private deposition, placing his testimony on the record. Hopefully, that will take away any incentive for Colby to hire anyone else in the future."

The fear and worry left Jessica's face and she smiled.

"It's over?" she whispered.

"Yes," he said. "It's over."

"And you," she said. "Will you be going back to Austin?"

"Are you kidding?" he asked. "I'm taking a leave of absence. Chasing around with you and that kid of ours plumb wore me out, woman."

Jessica laughed aloud, delighting in his smile and in the look in his eyes.

"I wasn't dreaming, was I?" she asked.

Diego's eyebrows drew together.

"I thought I remember hearing you say you loved me."

He grinned and leaned over, brushing a kiss against her mouth.

"You weren't dreaming," he said, grinning. "I love you more than life itself. And when you were so sick, I wanted to kick myself because I hadn't told you sooner. But I do love you, Jess. I've never stopped loving you. I was a lost, miserable man without you. And if I hadn't been so stubborn, it wouldn't have taken years for us to figure that out."

"We can't go back," she said, moving her head from side to side on the pillow.

"No way. From here on, Jess, it's going to be me and you and Tommy. I don't know where we'll end up—Austin, El Paso, or—"

"I don't care," she said, reaching forward for his kiss. "I don't care where we are, as long as we're together."

"That's one thing I can promise," he said, his voice tender. "We'll be together. Now that God has given us a second chance, I'm not going to waste it."

He took Jessica in his arms and kissed her slowly, sealing their love, this time forever.

BOOK YOUR PLACE ON OUR WEBSITE
AND MAKE THE
READING CONNECTION!

We've created a customized website just for our very
special readers, where you can get the inside scoop on
everything that's going on with Zebra, Pinnacle and
Kensington books.

When you come online, you'll have the exciting
opportunity to:

- View covers of upcoming books
- Read sample chapters
- Learn about our future publishing schedule
  (listed by publication month *and author*)
- Find out when your favorite authors will be visiting
  a city near you
- Search for and order backlist books from our
  online catalog
- Check out author bios and background information
- Send e-mail to your favorite authors
- Meet the Kensington staff online
- Join us in weekly chats with authors, readers and
  other guests
- Get writing guidelines
- AND MUCH MORE!

**Visit our website at
http://www.zebrabooks.com**

COMING IN FEBRUARY FROM
ZEBRA BOUQUET ROMANCES

#33 COMING HOME by Ann Josephson
__(0-8217-6485-3, **$3.99**) After her fiancé dies, quilt shop owner Althea Simmons promises herself that she'll never risk the pain of another loss . . . until she discovers a passion with sexy software designer Jared Cain she thought was long buried. Now Jared must set out to convince her that love is worth the gamble.

#34 THE COLORS OF LOVE by Vanessa Grant
__(0-8217-6486-1, **$3.99**) Beautiful Seattle artist Jamie Ferguson finds Dr. Alex Kent domineering and strangely gruff. But as she spends weeks painting his portrait, she discovers that his scowl hides a well of tenderness. It will be up to her to show him that the growing love they share is not only red-hot, but true blue—enduring, timeless, and simply meant to be.

#35 MAGGIE'S BABY by Colleen Faulkner
__(0-8217-6487-X, **$3.99**) Jarrett McKay was always prepared for the possibility that Maggie Turner might return someday and threaten to take their daughter away. What he never expected was the rush of emotion that sweeps him back to a time when he loved her desperately . . .

#36 COOKIES AND KISSES by Gina Jackson
__(0-8217-6488-8, **$3.99**) After his disastrous first marriage, Neil Rossi swore he'd never be wed again. But when he is threatened with a custody suit, he realizes he must find a perfect stepmom for his kids. Who better than his new pal, sweet and wholesome Taylor MacIntyre? The trouble is, Neil soon develops forever kind of feelings for his *temporary* Mrs.!

Call toll free **1-888-345-BOOK** to order by phone or use this coupon to order by mail.

Name _____

Address _____

City _____ State _____ Zip_____

Please send me the books I have checked above.

I am enclosing	$_____
Plus postage and handling*	$_____
Sales tax (in NY and TN)	$_____
Total amount enclosed	$_____

*Add $2.50 for the first book and $.50 for each additional book.
Send check or money order (no cash or CODs) to:
Kensington Publishing Corp., Dept. CO, 850 Third Avenue, New York, NY 10022
Prices and numbers subject to change without notice. Valid only in the U.S.
All books will be available 2/1/00. All orders subject to availability.
Visit our website at **www.kensingtonbooks.com**.